THE GIRL WHO CRIED WOLF

BELLA JAMES

Published by Accent Press Ltd 2016

Paperback ISBN: 9781786151926
Ebook ISBN: 9781786151742

PART ONE

PART ONE

CHAPTER ONE:

CALLING IN SICK?

You name it, I've done it.

I've had every ear, nose and throat infection known to man. I've lost countless aunties, uncles and grandparents. In fact, I think during Year 11 I made the amateur mistake of losing a particular grandparent more than once. A rather weary-looking tutor asked me, 'Anna, didn't you already lose your father's mother not long before last term's essays were due?'

If anyone finds it unethical using a loved one's demise to avoid handing in coursework, you won't be terribly impressed to know that before her actual death, the same granny's passing was also the reason I made it to Ayia Napa for Jules' eighteenth birthday instead of producing a paper on Shakespeare's sonnets. She managed a fairly decent spell of good health after that, until sadly being cremated a third and final time when Ashley in Year 12 had tickets for Rihanna.

Now I attend sixth form, a note from my oblivious mother no longer suffices. I have to do the unpleasantries by means of telephone, but I am perfectly happy to report that at the tender age of seventeen, I have this down to a fine art.

Essentially, the trick to a compelling 'calling in sick' is to really *believe* your afflictions. Sound effects are good, like holding six grapes in your cheek when feigning a dental emergency, but nothing beats the actual enactment. Heart and soul. When using the age-old stomach upset, actually *feel* the cramps. Hold your tummy and bend over slightly with imagined pain, then adopt a defeatist tone when you speak. Aim for suffering, with a hint of despair.

Of course, this only ever works on the school secretary, who doesn't really give a flying fuck whether you're ill or dying. Having said that, the non-judgemental answering machine is always a most welcome and sympathetic listener.

However, if you are one of those unfortunate souls whose sick call goes straight to Head of Year, you can forget about it. Once a term, they attend a secret seminar that enables them to detect the fakers immediately.

In such a circumstance, you must bite the bullet. Take a shower, haul on yesterday's un-ironed clothes, squeeze onto the bus with the other unfortunates, and go to school.

It was because of my atrocious attendance record of forty-six per cent that I received a summons to the dreaded School Welfare Officer, Maddy Nettleship. This mountain of a woman took one look at my extensive paperwork and proceeded to inform my suitably shocked mother of all my absences, making it compulsory that we attend an official appointment with a doctor to avoid suspension. Not a fabulous fictitious one who would diagnose all of my aforementioned ailments, either. An actual General Practitioner of Health, with certificates and probably a very cold stethoscope.

I looked over now at a drunk Jules, who sensibly left South Bank Campus after her final GCSE exam, and beckoned her to top up my glass. We have bravely made the sophisticated move from cider to my mother's expensive Chablis.

'I'll brave it out,' I tell my best friend. 'I'll say I have a weakened immune system, something both genetic *and* hereditary. I wish I had something grim. That would show them.'

She squinted at me through intoxicated eyes.

'Show them you're a lazy pisshead who can't be bothered to get up at six every morning.'

'Well, you'd know,' I slurred back at her, having expected a bit more sympathy from my so-called confidant.

Only Jules knew the true extent of my feigned illnesses as I struggled my way through English

Literature and Sociology. Last week we'd squealed with laughter at having left a drunken message recounting the sudden onset of hand, foot and mouth disease. The fact that we had just survived four days at Glastonbury went unmentioned, leaving us to focus on the truth that the body parts in question were incredibly sore and swollen.

I've actually not been quite so on-the-ball lately. I've let things slip – a combination of excessive fooling around and an abundance of late nights.

It's gone three in the morning and I have no idea how I'm to defend myself tomorrow. I've always had somewhat optimistic inclinations and I am truly hoping the doctor will be a like-minded soul. If I was in such a powerful position I would share conspirators' giggles with the shirkers who came in and tell them not to worry, that of course I could scribble something illegible on a form and tell their evil teachers not to be so insensitive to the stresses of teenage angst.

Jules is quoting something from our school handbook. I have no idea what she is talking about, possibly because, since the wine has run dry, we've made the desperate decision to drink my father's treasured port. I would never drink it sober, but I need oblivion. I need to forget that in five hours I will be showered and dressed. My teeth will be brushed until my gums bleed to hide the unmistakable breath of the three a.m. drinker. I will be standing outside the room of a doctor, who is undoubtedly going to contribute to my early exclusion from Year 13.

***

At precisely nine a.m., I had to bite the bullet and shuffle sheepishly through the door of a tiny office and plonk myself unsteadily into the patient's chair. I had managed to persuade Mother to wait outside.

Dr Braby, they call her. Just my luck to get an uncaring, probably never had a sick day ever, bespectacled jobsworth. I feel utterly sorry for myself. My saving grace is that I am definitely still a little bit pissed, and that has taken the edge off my morning's grim humiliation so far.

'I see that you've suffered Legionnaire's Disease on more than one occasion, Miss Winters. Extraordinary. Can you elaborate?'

At this point I shamefacedly muttered something about the mouldy tiles in the school shower block. A lone brain cell was ferociously scouring my memory bank for a snippet of info regarding the ailment, to no avail of course. I was high and dry and she knew it.

'You also suffer from chronic migraine, dizzy spells *and* gout?'

I try to muster up some indignation at this point because I actually do get a lot of headaches, which Jules tells me is a result of attempting to down one's body weight in peach cider every weekend.

'My headaches are awful,' I tell her truthfully. 'Sometimes they wake me up when I'm sleeping.'

She keeps tapping with irritating efficiency on the keyboard, seemingly oblivious to my solitary genuine complaint.

I looked at her a little more closely. Bespectacled, but by Gucci; she looked clean and well-groomed: a woman who looked better at forty-five than I ever would. She had sculpted, baby blonde hair that looked natural but could not possibly be unless her father was Nicky Clarke and her mother a Swedish supermodel.

'Did you hear me, Miss Winters? I asked who it was exactly that diagnosed your early menopause.'

I'm sure I saw the slightest hint of a smile playing at the corner of her coral painted lips. I relaxed a little. Sure, she had been seventeen herself a few decades ago. Sure, she could remember what it was like to put partying before the daily grind of pointless exams and coursework or trying to impress your reptilian tutors.

I gave her my most charming smile. Apparently this was a big mistake, as I received a lecture on the seriousness of our (when did it become me and her?) situation.

I decided the best way to handle this was to remain confident. I told her firmly that I'd had many allergies since birth, probably the result of an unpredictable and weakened immune system.

Perhaps this last statement was not the sole reason I spent the next forty-seven minutes being poked, prodded and downright violated.

***

I heard nothing from the doctor for seven days. Most of which were spent kicking myself and asking Jules questions such as 'How could I have been so stupid?' and 'How much do you get on the dole these days?' To which she replied rather bluntly with things like, 'Because you're *too* reckless' and 'About sixty-five quid.'

Even my partner in crime didn't have the decency to console me and tell me everything would be fine, that our Head of Year didn't have a leg to stand on. She should be telling me to sue him for unjust allegations and become a wealthy lady of leisure, dressing in Prada and Chanel. No, my teammate had become a little too pious for my liking. Usually the first to be thrilled by my cavalier attitude to all things regimented and conforming, 'Like, maybe going to school once in a while?' she now bleats.

This prim new attitude is more disconcerting than the impending report from Doctor Barbie. I referred to her as this twice in front of my friends during lunch break and only Miles sniggered. Miles, who still thinks 'Pull my finger' is funny. I know what's wrong with them; they think I've drawn too much attention to our happy camp.

Now that one of the unnoticeables has been singled out for a grilling, they think we'll all be dragged into the spotlight. Perhaps we were being paranoid, but certain teachers have been spotted lurking in the foyer, whispering and glancing in our direction at the canteen. None of us will be seen leafing through *Glamour* during assembly this week. We are still in the very back row behind the assistants and the wheelchair users, but now we're actually listening to the droning voices at the front of the school hall – not pretending to listen while texting and Tweeting, not mastering the art of falling asleep with our eyes open – actually listening.

The smallest of fish in Year 13 – once the blissfully inconspicuous bottom feeders in a sea of teachers and year leaders – have attracted the scrutinising gaze of the Great White: Mr Petri, Head of Sixth Form.

Everyone has heard about my drunken message. They're all privy to the fact our clique spent a long weekend at Glastonbury. They've seen the evidence. While I'm still the favoured target for most of the daggers fired by my peers, Miles is thankfully taking some of the heat for posting the incriminating photos on Facebook. They show none of us in a particularly generous light, although I secretly thought my hair looked really good in most of them, and was most thankful (not to mentioned incredibly surprised and relieved) for an experiment involving my sister's limited hairdressing skills and a bottle of L'Oreal Super Blonde the night before the festival.

I've always thought a woman's hair is her distinguishing feature. A lot can be said with style, colour and the length. The night before Glasto we had just finished watching *Girl with a Pearl Earring* starring Scarlett Johansson, a film based on the portrait. You don't see her hair till near the very end of the film, it's all tucked tightly under this bonnet she wears, so you've no idea how it looks. This really bothered me until Izzy told me that that was the point. It gave the character an air of mystery that inspired a masterpiece. 'Like burlesque,' she said. 'It's a visual seduction, a tease rather than giving too much away at once.'

I thought burlesque was more about making tassels swing in frantic circles from your boobs but considered what she said and sighed disconsolately.

'I'm not really into subtlety. A long, blonde mane catches the eye and that's job done. Anyway, Scarlett what's-her-face is so stunning she doesn't need hair. I do.'

Having never liked my dark blonde tresses, I passed Izzy the bleach...

Needless to say, despite the successful experiment, I've had a dreadful week since then and just wish someone at school would fall pregnant or catch chlamydia – anything to take the heat off *us*. No one knew we existed until this sorry affair was exposed, and now the teachers think we're a bunch of cider louts being influenced by either a raging hypochondriac or an unmotivated imbecile.

CHAPTER TWO:

THE MAD HATTER

My *mother* received a letter from Dr Braby seven days after our first meeting. I skilfully intercepted it, wanting to keep its contents to myself for the time being. It said that following her assessment of my health and fitness, she had referred me to a Mr Raj at the Milton Keynes General Hospital, Friday, 23rd September. How very strange, I thought, because obviously *I* knew that there was nothing wrong with me.

Perhaps she was punishing me in some sort of 'Boy Who Cried Wolf' way and I would have to humour her. Another seven days of waiting and I'm definitely beginning to feel a little apprehensive. I'd guessed that the two possible outcomes of our initial appointment were a) I would receive a warning to the effect of needing to improve my attendance at school, or b) I would be suspended. I did not foresee being sent to hospital to see a Mr Raj. Who the hell was he, anyway?

Later that day, Jules and I Googled him. Up comes his picture from the hospital website. He's dark skinned, in his late fifties perhaps, with a serious expression but reassuringly kind eyes.

'It says hear he specializes in neurology.'

'What in the world might that be?'

'Sexual diseases,' pipes up Miles, whom I look at in horror.

Obviously it was the reaction he had hoped for. He goes on to inform me that neurology is the study of sex-related diseases, primarily gonorrhoea and syphilis.

'Shut up, Miles, just because you've got pubic lice doesn't mean everyone else has. It's to do with the brain, Anna,' said Jules.

'She's sending me to see a shrink?!'

I slam down the laptop and put my head in the fold of my arms on the table.

'This is beyond a joke. Now they think I have psychological problems ... because I've tried to blag a couple days off school here and there?'

I don't see Jules snort but I hear her.

'I mean it's *normal* to hate exams, isn't it? They're the ones who need their heads tested. Not me.'

I am angry now, and beginning to sense imminent disaster. A dark feeling creeps slowly over me. It's still there as I'm called into Mr Raj's office the following week.

'Anna Winters? Please come in and have a seat.' He points to an enormous wing-back chair facing his desk, as he sits opposite, eyeing me with interest.

'Are you a psychiatrist?' I ask, holding his gaze with my chin held up defiantly.

A hint of a smile and then, 'No, Anna. I'm a neurologist; I specialize in the workings of the brain, among other things.'

'Oh.' I take this in while I literally have to pull myself onto the chair and scooch back. The chair is so huge I feel like Alice in Wonderland, when she is very small and the world is getting bigger around her.

'Dr. Braby has asked me to meet with you today. She is studying neurology also, part time, and she has a keen interest in all things brain!'

I feel like I'm missing something, so I say nothing.

'During your physical examination and having ...' He looked down at his notes at this point. '... attempted to separate fact from fiction ... she picked up on a few things that may warrant further investigation.'

He takes off his glass and comes round to my side of the desk, leaning against it and folding his arms.

'I need to ask you some questions, some of which may seem strange but it is of the utmost importance that you answer them as accurately and as honestly as you can.'

'OK.' I try to sound as bored as possible but my voice comes out with a quiet quiver. Something is not right here, and I'm still convinced that he is psychoanalyzing me.

'What is today's date? Including the year.'

That throws me a little; I was expecting him to ask me how I felt about my father.

'Erm, the twenty something of September, 2015.'

He leans behind him and marks something on a piece of paper.

'And who is the Deputy Prime Minister?'

I look behind me at this point, expecting to see Jules with Miles, sniggering at their practical joke. Or maybe Ashton Kutcher.

I offer him a cautious 'Ed Miliband?' as I do not know, and never have known, who the Deputy Prime Minister is, but I have *heard* of Ed Miliband because Jules says her Uncle Rupert looks like him.

'And tell me your date of birth, including the year.'

Nice and easy. I start with confidence. 'The first of September ...' then my mind just goes blank. Of course I know what year I was born. It is there somewhere but the information will not reach my mouth. He watches me struggling, seemingly unconcerned that he has me so thrown and nervous

I can't remember my own bloody birth year.

'I'm seventeen!' I blurt out crossly, and now it is my turn to fold my arms. I glare at him, convinced he is completely out of his mind.

Mr Raj places some paper in front of me and asks me to draw some shapes and then continues to ask more ridiculous questions.

He shines a light in my eyes, particularly my right one, and does the knee-tapping thing that makes your leg stick out. I'm subjected to similar tests to those Dr Braby carried out. Lying flat, tummy prodded, asking me to lift my legs in turn ... squeeze his finger (I silently pray he doesn't have the same sense of humour as Miles), smile, half smile, stick your tongue out, and it just goes on and on. God, Mr Petri must really hate me.

I had not even noticed the door opening, but as he asks me to sit up and swing my legs over the side of the bed, I see a plump nurse sitting a little way to the left of us. She smiles at me.

'Anna, if you could take your jumper off, please, I need to listen to your chest.'

A cold wave of despair washes over me as I realise I'm wearing my sexy lace bra, the one with a sparkly red heart over each nipple. "Damn you, Boux Avenue" is my only anguished thought as I pull my jumper off and stare furiously at the nurse's sensible shoes.

When it's finally all over I find myself back in Alice in Wonderland's chair.

'Dr Braby was right; you seem to have some weakness in your left side, along with headaches. You say you wake up with them sometimes?'

I nod.

'I'm also seeing a little swelling on one of your optical discs ...'

He continues to look at his notes and starts tapping away on his keyboard.

'Do you ever suffer from *deja vu*, Anna?'

'Didn't you ask me that earlier?' I smile but he carries on, ignoring my hilarious joke.

'Do you ever feel dizzy or uncoordinated?'

'I don't know.'

I'm starting to feel very hot, not to mention uncomfortable and I cannot tell him how much I want to get out of here and down to the Whistling Duck where Jules and Miles are waiting for me.

'Mood swings?'

I flick my hair over my shoulder and tell him, 'I'm a woman, Mr Raj; it is my prerogative to have mood swings.' My returning feistiness brings with it a little comfort.

Taking his glasses off again, the stranger opposite me tells me that he is booking me some scans and further eyesight and hearing tests.

'Why do I need them? I'm not really ill, you know. I've just been a bit under the weather. You know what it's like ... a few too many sick days, but do I really need a full MOT? Surely you must have real patients to see to? I'll get out of your hair. Sorry to have wasted so much of your time.'

I go to shake his hand but his arms remain folded, leaving me hanging, so I clamp my arm back to my side.

'Anna, some of these tests are highlighting factors that could relate to brain malfunction. I don't want to alarm you, and it may be nothing serious, but you need to attend these investigative procedures. I'll send you the information you'll need for your scan then we'll meet again when I have your results.'

He heads back round to his side of the desk and sits down, replaces his spectacles, and bids me a rather curt, 'Good day.'

I take my cue to leave and jump down from the chair with pleasure. I exit his room, department, and hospital as fast as my shaky legs will allow me.

***

It takes four ciders to convince myself that everything is going to be fine. Jules and Miles laughed uproariously when I lifted my jumper and showed them the bra I was wearing. They agreed with enthusiasm that this was all a wicked plot to teach me a lesson, and by cider number six I realized that of course Miles was right. Mr Raj was not a real doctor; he was an actor hired by Petri to enhance this elaborate scheme.

I spent the next week trying to convince myself that everything was going to be all right. Sleep became impossible, so I perfected a regime of raiding my mother's wine stash each night, only to pass out and wake around dawn with an increasingly torturous headache. I existed on paracetamol and the odd slice of toast, occasionally supplemented with a can or two of Red Bull to get me through the abomination of school work. Had I known what was to come, I need not have bothered showing up for my classes ever again.

It only took one rather frightening CT scan and a similarly disconcerting MRI to convince Mr Raj that I had a grade-three tumour, nestled snugly in the frontal lobe of my brain. Everything that I had attributed to too little sleep and too much alcohol was in fact caused by a malignant mass of cells, growing steadily with each day.

The shaking, the dizziness, the headaches, forgetfulness, tiredness, and numbness were not caused by self-anaesthetising with cider and the occasional joint. I had cancer.

'I'm sorry, what?'

He looks at me steadily while handing out this death sentence and the plump nurse sits solidly to my left, offering to hold my hand. I ignore her entirely and direct my gaze back to him. The room gets smaller. I feel as though I'm struggling to breathe as he asks me if there is anyone I would like him to call. I feel very sick, and as if on cue, the tumour causing my headaches sends a marching band through my brain, an excruciating stamp on every nerve just in case I did not get the message.

You have cancer! It pounded into me.

I do not fully remember the next few minutes. I wished I hadn't excluded my mother. I suppose I cried with shock and fear. The nurse ignored my protests and put her arms around me. It was a surprisingly comforting gesture. If she had dallied about or been the slightest bit hesitant I would have imploded, but she held me firmly and stroked my back with confident hands.

'Will I die?'

He must dread this question, but he was well prepared.

'Anna, this has come as a terrible shock to you but you must take heed that we are treating your illness with an aim to cure. There have been many exciting developments in this field over recent years. We will do everything we can to treat you, and I can assure you the oncology and neurosurgery team at Milton Keynes Hospital are second to none.'

Himself included, I supposed, as he said the last part with pride.

'So I won't die?'

I wouldn't let him wriggle off the hook quite so easily.

At this point, the door opened and I heard a faintly familiar voice. 'May I come in?'

I turn to see Dr Braby hesitating and it's all I can do to stop myself launching at her. All my hate focuses in her direction, and with one look at me she actually takes a step back.

'This is your fault,' I hiss. 'I was fine until I came to see you, now I have a brain tumour! Tell her!'

I look at Mr Raj, looking less confident and probably more familiar with patients who need sympathy and comfort after this sort of news. Not me. I've always been an angry person and quick to find someone to blame. Well, here was the person. Miss Perfect was done up to the nines for work, and for what? Just to interfere and ruin lives with her examinations and fascination with 'all things brain'. I started shouting at her, words I cannot remember. I may have called her a slut, at which point Mr Raj slammed his hand on his desk, making us all jump, and Braby left, closing the door swiftly behind her.

'Did that make you feel better?'

Actually it did, but his face had gone very red so I said nothing. Angry men unnerve me.

'*I* invited Dr. Braby to our meeting. She is very learned in this field and I thought you may want to *thank* her for alerting us to your illness. Lord only knows how long it would have taken you to realize you were ill. By which time your condition could have been so much harder to treat.'

I cannot help but feel desperately sorry for myself. Now I'm being told off? The nurse, who had removed her arm from me when I started shouting, professionally changes the subject and suggests we discuss treatment and focus on that for now. Mr Raj smiles gratefully and she blushes. He tells me he would look further at my scan results before deciding on the next course of action.

'The tumour is not in the most desirable place so it is likely we shall start a course of radio and possibly chemotherapy before attempting surgery. This could reduce the mass and make matters more promising for us.'

'Not the most desirable place?' I am left wondering in what world there is a desirable location for a brain tumour. I sigh and, with that, the dark cloud settles itself contentedly above me.

***

It has been a little over a month, but I have not entirely accepted the fact that my old life has finished; that I now belong to this nightmare – a new world of pain, fear and desolation. I have experienced levels of pain I did not know existed, and I've had treatments you would not wish upon your most hated enemy.

November's early dusk creeps into the room in which I now reside, and to my left I hear my mother snoring gently, her posture awkward in the visitor's chair. I feel a sudden rush of love I've not felt in long while. For the first time since my illness struck, I was not thinking about myself. I was sad for her. She had never been very tactile with me or my younger sister, Isabel. There had never been any of the all-enveloping bear hugs that came naturally to most parents. Mother would pat us gently on the shoulder if we brought home a good school report, or give us an occasional brusque kiss on the cheek if she was feeling really affectionate.

We had always been cared for, I suppose. A little spoilt, really, with bedrooms crammed full of dolls and toys, dresses that matched shoes and ribbons that matched dresses. I didn't want to feel angry at her any more. She barely left my bedside now.

I pulled the blanket away from my legs and, manoeuvring around my drip-stand, tucked it gently around her. I wanted to close the window at the far end of the room but I was too tired. A cold autumn breeze blew the thin curtains back and forth in a ghostly dance.

I opened my eyes sometime later and Mother was fussing around the bed, tidying up. The blue blanket was back over my legs and the window was firmly closed.

She did not exactly stroke my head, but she sort of patted it the way a person might pet their friend's snarling Chihuahua when they're secretly terrified but do not want to seem rude.

'The doctor is on his way, Anna. We should be ready for him.'

Mr Raj walked in right on cue. Despite having my own room, there is no privacy here. Your body becomes hospital property. I've woken up several times during the night to find a nurse is injecting something into my stomach. No explanation, no 'Perhaps we should wake her first and see if she minds being stabbed with whatever this is.'

In here I was no longer Anna Winters; I was female patient in room C. Brain tumour.

Mr Raj pulled the visitor's chair towards me with a piercing scrape and sat down. Mum hovered behind him, then to his left, and eventually plonked herself down at the bottom of the bed. I could hear her breathing.

'How are you feeling, Anna?'

The old me would have had a thousand sarcastic quips to offer him, but now my mouth felt too dry, my mind too cloudy. 'OK,' I mumbled.

'I have the results from your last scan and I'm afraid it's not good news. The chemo does not seem to be working. This will be your last session, and in a week we may let you go home while we plan the next stage in your treatment.'

'Aren't I too sick to go home?'

'I talked to your mother earlier and she will take care of you at home for a little while. I think being away from here will do you good. Try to regain your appetite, get plenty of rest, and we'll we see where we are then.'

'Am I going home to die?'

I heard my mother let out a tiny cry but I was sick of beating around the bush.

'Anna, look at me. You are a very stubborn and determined girl. I strongly advise you to use this to your advantage and be determined to get through this. I have practiced medicine for many years and have seen people with worse prospects get well again. But we *will* need to operate to remove the tumour before it causes any further damage. I would have liked it to be smaller but that's not happening, so we will work with what we've got. The operation will carry risks; I've explained those to you.'

'Tell me again.' I wasn't going to make this easy on him and I wanted the gory details. I was beyond terrified, and making this man feel uncomfortable was the only power I had. 'I have a right to know *exactly* all the risks.'

'Anna, please try to stay strong.'

'Tell me!' I shouted, making him jump. Ha, that got him. It pleased me to see that he looked shocked and annoyed. It really ticks me off that some doctors choose to behave like they are so above you. They tell you things on a-need-to-know basis and I was not having it. It was my tangled brain and for me this was life or death. For him it was just another tricky operation that afterwards he could literally wash his hands of, saying he'd tried.

He composed himself and looked me right in the eye. 'As you know, the tumour is large and growing. It is located in a dangerous place and we can't be sure till we operate how close it is to the cerebral lining. Its position also increases the risk of a haemorrhage. The operation has a thirty-seven per cent complete success rate. It can commonly cause paralysis, speech impairment, memory loss ...'

Thank God he'd stopped talking as he sees my face and my mother's sobs grow louder.

'Anna, people do survive these operations and make good recoveries. Please focus on that, and, my team will do their very best for you. I need you strong before we can attempt anything, so for once listen to your mother –' (he seemed to know a bit too much here. I glared at her) '– and let her take care of you.' He paused and looked at his chart. 'I see you've lost a great deal of hair.'

Where the hell had that come from? I reached my hand up to my head and realized I had been too out of it lately to notice.

'I'm sorry, does that bother you?' I said heatedly. 'Would you like me to hop on the bus to the nearest Vidal Sassoon and see if they can do something with it?' I grabbed a few strands that came away in my hand and held them in front of my face while Mum cried gently. It angered me even more that she was crying. *I'm* the one who's losing my hair, my mind, my life. I started to shout at her hysterically, telling her to stop looking at me like that. 'Get out! Get out! GET OUT!'

At that point I saw someone tall standing in the doorway watching me, and through a blur of tears, I started screaming. A nurse pushed past them and tried to hold me down and I felt like I wanted to explode with rage. I was crying so hard it was difficult to breathe. Another person entered the room with a small tray of medication. But the fight had left as quickly as it came, and I had no strength left as she held my arm down and administered a now redundant sedative.

Chapter Three:

A LITTLE KINDNESS

I must have been out for a while, because when I open my eyes they are all gone. My sister is next to me, and I see she is reading one of those awful celebrity magazines we pretend to despise but secretly love.

'It says here that Taylor Swift weighs eight stone seven.'

At the sound her voice, I try to pull myself out of the drug-induced sleep.

'That's seven pounds more than you.'

For the next few moments, I forget I have cancer.

'I'm thinner than Taylor Swift?'

'According to your hospital records.'

'Let me see that.' I snatch the clipboard that should have been hooked on the bed rail from her grip. 'God, it's true. Annabelle Winters, height, five foot six, weight ... eight stone. I've never been eight stone! I'm positively gaunt.' I almost cry with happiness. 'Who else is in there?'

'Cheryl Cole, no make-up. Kim Kardashian in frock-horror shocker, and Rhianna, before and after the maple syrup diet.'

'Ooh, let me see.' I grab the magazine off her and we enjoy a few more minutes analysing who has had Botox and who needs it.

Sometime later, Dr Braby sticks her head round the corner.

'Are you feeling better, Anna? It certainly sounds like it.'

She said it nicely but there was a tone to her voice I could not quite place. Possibly fear.

'Do you mind if I talk to you for a few minutes?'

Isabel jumped up like a rocket saying she needed to go to the café and did I want some chocolate brought back?

'No thanks, but maybe some juice?' I had learned that if I added a drink on the end of 'no, thank you' every time I was offered something to eat, I was less likely to get a lecture.

Dr Barbie was having none of it. 'Bring Anna some fruit, please, Isabel.' She looked back to me. 'How will your body repair itself if you don't give it the tools to do so? You need a little protein, vitamins and carbohydrates to get well again.'

She continued to drone on about fats and minerals so I rolled my eyes at Izzy, expecting her to pull a face also. We hated being told what to eat, and much preferred diet and starvation. But she nodded along with Dr Braby, agreeing that I needed to eat more, and that she'd bring me some bananas for folic acid and berries for antioxidants.

I felt doomed as Izzy left the room and closed the door behind her.

'Mr Raj told me how upset you were earlier.'

'So would you be if you just found out that you've suffered the worst, most terrifying weeks of your life for nothing. That it didn't work but hey, look on the bright side; you've lost all your hair and you can no longer eat or drink without throwing up so let's just look forward to the major brain surgery you probably won't survive and be happy, shall we?'

Dr Braby took off her expensive glasses and looked at me. I thought her lovely eyes seemed watery and she suddenly seemed rather young and soft.

I let out a big sigh and tried hard not to start crying. 'Please don't start being nice. It might make me throw up again.'

She smiled and said, 'Actually, I wanted to talk to you about your hair. Don't start shouting at me just yet, and try to remember that I've spent a lot of time with women who've been through this so *maybe* I can help.'

I wanted desperately to tell her to fuck off but I do not speak to people like that, so I said nothing. I stared furiously at a freckle on one of my hands instead.

'Your hair will grow back, Anna, probably a lot faster than you think, but for the next few months I want you to be able to face yourself and what's happening to you.'

I felt some consolation that she seemed to think that I might still be here in a few months, until I looked down and saw she was holding a hand mirror.

'I know that you've taken down the mirror in the bathroom, and you won't let anyone touch your hair, but if you want it to grow back healthy, we need to cut it properly. I've brought some lotion that helps regrowth.'

'Anna, I know you hate me. I've brought you nothing but bad news since we met, but please try to let me help.'

She was right. I did hate her, but part of me was curious to see what it was she had in mind. How awful did I actually look? The fact that almost everyone winced when they first came in to see me was not a good sign. A few weeks ago I did take down the bathroom mirror, Barbie was right about that.

I had made the mistake of looking into it after being sick through the night, and never mind the cancer, I nearly died right there and then. My face was unpleasantly gaunt, and there were blue and black circles around my eyes like dark bruises.

Eyebrows and eyelashes gone, skin an ashen grey, but worse than any of that, worse than the stranger's face looking back at me through hollow eyes, was my not so long ago Super Blonde hair.

I only had small tufts near my forehead and round the skull, then some long, thin straggly strands near the nape of my neck and my ears. They had all brought me various bandanas and wigs since then, but I was not in the mood. I had always worn make-up, and aimed for immaculacy. I loved moisturising my skin and highlighting my features. Kohl around the eyes, blusher to the apples of my cheeks, and I have very rarely been seen without lip gloss. It was the part of being female I loved the most. The bubble baths, the body oils, the hair perfume. And now look at me. No, if I was going to look like the walking dead I might as well do it right. I could not see any way back to myself and it terrified me more than the cancer.

I took the mirror from above the wash basin and rested it gently but firmly behind the sink unit, glass facing the wall. I remember going to bed that night and praying to God I would not wake up.

'I've brought you some things.' Dr Braby's strident voice broke through my thoughts.

I must admit I was more than a little enticed when she placed some rather expensive-looking bags on the tray in front me. I saw Ralph Lauren and what looked like a Chanel powder compact.

I tried my best to look nonchalant, and sighed dramatically. 'If you must.'

I felt hugely self-conscious as she snipped away at the sparse strands of hair and cut them short. But she chatted as she snipped and it was starting to feel better. This woman was so bloody sure of herself it was hard to believe she did not know exactly what she was doing.

'That's better already,' she told me, using a huge make-up brush to dust the hairs off me as if we were in a salon. 'Izzy told me she brought you some toiletries weeks ago but you've never even looked at them.'

'In that cupboard.' I pointed to where I had stuffed the bag, thinking I was too miserable for my old luxuries. They belonged to another life.

'Here, have a look.'

I opened the lovely Ted Baker bag and ooh'd and aah'd for a while at its contents. How could I have missed out on this, and have not even thanked Izzy?

All of my favourite things: a bottle of Chloé perfume (almost new), some Max Factor lip crayons, Olay cleansing wipes, and a Clinique moisturiser. There were more treasures in the side compartment; YSL Touche Éclat, and a large tube of Benefit lip gloss.

I was beginning to think this had all been planned. How did Dr Braby know Izzy tried to give me these things and I had all but thrown them back at her?

My hands were a little shaky so the good doctor ordered me to lie back against the propped up pillows, and can you imagine that I actually let her cleanse my skin with the wipes? It felt tingly and fresh against my dry face. She gently massaged and moisturized with Clinique and it felt a little like a spa treatment. I felt relaxed and maybe a less afraid. Who knows, one day I might get better, maybe my hair would grow back and I could find a way to be me again. Dangerous optimism.

She dabbed the concealer around my eyes and finished off with a dusting of her own Chanel powder and a tiny bit of bronzer.

'You look so different, Anna.'

I didn't really believe her, but ever hopeful, I found myself smiling back at her.

'That's the first time you've ever smiled at me properly. It's so much nicer than being scowled and shouted at.' She was reaching into the larger bag and pulling out some bronze tissue paper. 'I bought this in Italy a long time ago. I haven't worn it – it never suited me – but I was clearing out my drawers and I … Well, I thought you might like it.'

Looking a little awkward, she pulled out a silk Ralph Lauren head scarf, cream with gold buckles and horseshoes. It was beautiful. I let the silky material glide through my bony fingers.

'I couldn't,' I began to say, but she swiftly

folded the scarf a few times (she had clearly done this before) and gently placed it over me, covering my forehead, tying it low at the back so the two ends fell over my shoulders. Then she held up the mirror.

'Maybe you're ready to look at yourself again.'

I breathed deeply and took the mirror, gasping when I saw the reflection. I still looked very different but there was no mistaking the girl looking back at me. The one I thought had already died.

Dr Braby left soon after, and I almost thanked her as she started to walk through the door. Instead I asked, 'Do you give all your patients silk head scarves?'

'No,' she replied simply. 'But technically, you're not my patient. I seem to have adopted you.'

I spent the next ten minutes alone, growing ever more critical of the girl in the mirror. I actually thought I looked sort of pretty. A little fragile, but it suited me. It was the eyebrows and lashes that let me down, that made me look ill, not to mention the fact that under the scarf I had about as much hair as a newly hatched chick. I smudged a little grey pencil around my eyes, applied some lip gloss, and was trying desperately to be positive when Isabel walked back in. She was carrying what appeared to be a market stall worth of fruit. Looking a little taken aback, she dropped the fruit on the table (and floor) and sat next to me, leaning in for a closer look.

I had to ask her the question I would be too afraid to ask anyone else. Doctors, Jules, my parents ... I knew she would tell me the truth; she could be brutal and knew I did not need to be patronized. Izzy had seen me at my best and now my very worst. She knew all my secrets. We had always been a little competitive – she was naturally pretty in a way I envied. She envied my flair, and my incessant need to take centre stage had always riled her. We loved and fought each other and I knew as I lay pathetic and spent in that hospital bed, she could make or break me.

'How do I look?'

Her grey eyes never left mine, nor did they waver for a second.

'Like Scarlett Johansson.'

And that, ladies and gentleman, is why God created sisters.

***

I had just turned four when Izzy was born, but I still remember the events surrounding her arrival rather well. It began with my parents sitting me down in our grand living room and talking to me about my cousins Cher and Natasha.

'You know that they're sisters, darling? Well, how would you feel about having a little brother or sister to play with?'

Hmmph. This was a tricky one. My young mind whirled around the possibilities of this new concept. For one, I did always feel a little bit of an outsider when we were all together. Tash and Cher had a bond that reminded me of an exclusive club, or a secret that I was not quite privy to. On the other hand, they did spend a lot of time fighting like monsters, and I often became the one to pair up with after such arguments. They always made up though, and we would be back to square one, me desperately trying to join in with their whispered giggling and jokes I did not quite get.

Natasha was the eldest, and she seemed to get the better deal. If there were toys or sweets to be shared, she always got to do the dealing out sixty-forty. She made all the important decisions, like who would be the princess and who the servant, who got to play with Malibu Barbie and which of us was left with a bereft-looking Sindy (usually me).

Of course, with my parents waiting for my answer, these musings flashed by me in a heartbeat. When you are so young, you don't agonize over decisions, you decide instinctively. The dissecting of every single detail comes much later in life – along with the paranoid fear of making the wrong choices that have often led me to a sleepless night.

'Will I be the oldest one?'

'Well, yes, darling, you were born first so you'll

be four years older. You'll be able to help look after her.'

'Then yes,' I decided firmly. 'We'll call her Tulip as well.' My only experience thus far of taking care of something was the tender love and care I proffered to my darling dwarf rabbit, Tulip. She lived contentedly in our garden shed, with an outdoor run when the weather was good.

Apart from my fascination with my mother's ever-growing bump, I do not remember giving the new baby much more thought until the day she was born.

My mother ended a lovely outing rather suddenly, and took me to my grandparents' house, telling me to be good and wait for her. Something about buying me ice cream was mentioned, but even then I knew placation when I heard it. I begged her to take me with her, but she left me crying at the front door and never came back as promised.

'She said she would be back before bedtime,' I complained to Grandad that afternoon.

'Well, Anna, Lillian will be home when she's home, won't she? Won't be long now, I'm sure. Run along and fetch Grandad a bottle of beer from Granny, and I'll help you make Tulip another daisy chain.'

I felt certain something bad was happening and did not like him calling my mother by her actual name, but I went inside to find Grandma anyway.

Tulip did need another daisy chain – I think she had eaten the last one.

Grandma looked very worried and sad all evening but if I asked why she had been crying she told me not to be silly and said, 'Grandmas don't cry, darling. They're always happy and if we ever do cry, they are tears of joy. Don't you worry about that.'

I can't have looked convinced because she finished her drink and tickled my tummy until I cried lots of happy tears.

The following day, the phone rang and, afterwards, Grandad walked into the living room, beaming, and said, 'Well, my dear, you have a new granddaughter. Seven pounds and three ounces. Anna, you have a brand new baby sister!'

'Did she get her at the shops, Grandad?'

He laughed softly and plonked me on his lap. 'That's right, my little treasure, she went to the shops and swapped that great big bump in her tummy for a beautiful little girl for you to play with.' He chuckled again and downed the last of his celebratory beer.

Izzy was born on a Friday, but she was not brought home until nearly a week later. I was excited to see her, but had especially missed my mother, who had thought it was best if I stayed at home rather than going into hospital to see her. I had never been apart from her for so long and when I saw her walk through the front door, I ran straight into her arms.

But something *was* wrong; she had a huge cut along her forehead and a bandage on her arm. Dad was carrying a baby basket behind her. He looked terribly angry and did not acknowledge me at all.

'Hello, angel.' My mother bent down and hugged me as best she could. She held me tightly then stood back while Dad placed the bassinet on the settee beside us. 'Don't worry, Anna. Mummy just fell over. Come and say hello to Isabel.'

I was still deeply shocked to see my beautiful mother with bruises, but she did sound OK and I could not resist a peek at my new sister. I leaned over and there she was, wrapped up and pink-faced. I remember looking at her for a long time while the grown-ups fussed and got my mother settled. 'I wanted to call you Tulip like my bunny,' I told her, and gently put my hand near hers, a little afraid to touch her just yet. To my absolute delight, she reached up with her tiny fingers and grabbed my hand. 'Mummy, look! MUMMY! She's holding my hand!' I desperately wanted someone to see, to share the moment with me, but when I turned around I saw my dad leaving the house with a suitcase and Grandma with her head in her hands, crying more happy tears.

***

I remember Isabel coming home, but the years following are hazier. I know my father worked away for much of the time. I could often hear Mother crying in her room, so I supposed they had argued and he had left, but she would always give me the same response. 'Your father and I are just fine, Anna. I don't know where you get these things. You know he sells antiques all over the world; of course he couldn't be in two places at once.' The conversation would end with something like, 'God, your sister never asks these bloody questions!'

She got more and more bad-tempered as the years went by, and the beautiful, joyful mother of my childhood was a long way from the miserable, bitter-faced shell we had lived with since.

Don't get me wrong, my mother was still extremely beautiful. She was strikingly tall and fashionably slim – she barely ate so couldn't really be anything else. She had piercing green eyes which looked striking with her long blonde hair.

Her hair was usually pulled back into a conservative chignon, but the few times I had seen it worn loose, Mother really became exquisite. A little frown line had appeared between her eyebrows over the years, but other than that it was hard to find fault with her appearance. Lillian's character, however, was far from charming.

Before Isabel was born I remember her laughing so much more. She was always a little reserved but affectionate in her own way. Izzy and I were wary of her mood swings, and although she tried to disguise them, she was short-fused and liked to spend a great deal of time alone. We were often packed off to our grandparents' for the weekend, even during the rare occasions my father came home.

We never minded going to Grandma's. During the day we would run wild in the huge garden, and were not told to stay clean and make sure our hair was tidy. There were no designer dresses and ribbons to spoil anyway at Grandma's. As soon as we got there, Gran would pack them into a drawer and give us the clothes she had made especially for us: fabulous denim dungarees with big, red flower-shaped buttons. She would take our long hair down from its braids and tell us stories about Rapunzel and Sleeping Beauty.

Evenings were exciting. Grandma and Grandad drank little bottles of beer while we watched game shows and Izzy and I would entertain ourselves by building fortresses with the empty bottles. Looking back now I suppose they did drink too much. It came to a head one weekend when Izzy was eight and I was twelve and we helped ourselves to the 'special juice' that Gran told us was only for her and Grandad. But it was bright orange and fruity and I couldn't resist sneaking into the kitchen while they watched their shows and daring Izzy to try some. That was another great thing about having a sister; she was like the queen's taster. Anything I wasn't sure of, she tried it first. Izzy scooped a cup into the big glass bowl and took a little sip. She scrunched her cute face up.

'It's sort of sweet and funny tasting.'

'Have some more!' I egged her on, delighted that she was such a daredevil.

'I don't want to,' she whined and pulled the face she made right before crying.

'OK, baby face. I'll try it.' That seemed to cheer her up, and she scooped in to fill the cup up to the brim. I considered pretending to try it by spitting it back into the cup; she was so gullible I knew she would fall for it. But the truth was I *wanted* to try some. I had noticed every time adults drank, they got louder and sort of giggly. 'Tipsy', my gran would say.

'Bottom's up!' I said, and drank the whole cup. I knew I was showing off but Izzy looked so impressed I asked for another. And another. At first I liked the feeling, I was a little light-headed and starting being very silly, making Izzy laugh. Then of course I started to feel unpleasantly dizzy, and eventually began to throw up. I can't remember how many cups I had drunk when my grandparent's came rushing in, but I remember the look on their faces was so frightening I began to shake and cry hysterically. Grandad scooped me up and the last memory I have of that evening is being bundled into the back of a car and my little sister's frightened face at the dining room window, her lips mouthing my name.

I woke up in a hospital bed the next day, and my mother was beside me. Her eyes were red and she looked like she might start yelling, so I started to cry first and said sorry over and over. She held me in her arms and told me it wasn't my fault. We didn't stay at my grandparent's house after that until we were much older. My father started to come home at weekends and Izzy and I got on with our lives as children do.

I sometimes wonder if that could be the reason my mum is so cold to Grandma. But my grandparents loved us so much, and surely everyone is allowed one mistake? They didn't have alcohol around us again until very recently, so they had learned their lesson. I guessed that our mother was (as usual) looking for another reason to be judgmental and grim.

***

When I look out the window of my hospital room, I wonder how time can pass so quickly. It seems like only yesterday we were children, and Izzy would hold tightly on to my hand as we walked through the meadow to see the dapple grey pony Father had surprised us with one summer's afternoon. I close my eyes, praying to be returned to those happier times, where neither of us had heard of this illness and our only troubles were making flowers stay in Starlight's mane.

CHAPTER FOUR:

LOVE (IN THE TIME OF CHEMO)

The following few days were a little rough. Mr Raj came to see me the day after my hysterical outburst, said I looked better and seemed like he meant it. He told me they would be reducing my medication steadily over the next few days and that I should be able to go home a week on Friday, but coming off such high doses of medicine would take a temporary toll on my already weakened body. He mentioned nausea, headaches and aching joints, but I assured him I would be fine – Anything to get me out of the hospital for a while.

It had been decided that I would stay with my grandparents while in respite from treatment. I was getting increasingly distant towards my mother, and every time something went wrong I found a way to blame her. This was hardly fair, but I was tired and emotional, and I wanted to be in my grandma's cosy home with the big oak table, the wood burner, and those delicious smells enticing everyone to the kitchen. Even Lillian had to agree I would hardly regain my appetite over her offerings of microwave meals and endless rounds of toast with various toppings.

Izzy was more than a bit put out, but she had to be at school anyway, so she gave in on the condition that she could come up to visit every evening. So now I had to get through the next few days and I would be free again. Free from the drugs, the drip-stand that followed me everywhere, the probing staff, and the sleepless nights.

***

It was so much easier said than done. I spent the following day drifting in and out of consciousness, going from being hot and feverish to so cold that my bones themselves felt frozen. I finally found sleep in the early hours, but it was panicky, edgy, rather than restful.

I woke up to see a rather tall, incredibly bald man standing in front of me, not looking at all well. He looked old and frail but could not have been much more than twenty.

I couldn't manage words. My mind felt like cotton wool and I couldn't work out where I was or what was going on. I fought the urge to laugh at him. When I used to get stoned with a friend from our village it felt a lot like this. My thoughts were floating in front of me, but when I tried to grab them they slipped away.

I may have grunted at him.

'I'm Michael.' He was rearranging the contents of my bedside table. 'I walked past and heard you knock these over. Just thought I'd check someone hadn't hurt themselves.'

I had no idea what he was talking about. I vaguely remembered that I was in hospital, that something was very wrong, but I could not string anything together to make sense.

I tried to bring this man into focus. No hair. No eyebrows. He looked like he was very unfortunate indeed. I recognised my illness in his drawn and weary features, but there was something strange about the way he was making me feel as I stared harder. He was coming closer, sitting down beside me. Why was he straightening my blankets?

Cancer leaves a recognisable imprint, but it had failed to steal the sparkle from his eyes. He had intense grey-blue eyes in a handsome face with a chiselled jawline Michelangelo may have masterminded. The way he was looking at me was making me nervous. My head ached and I felt weak and wretched. But here was this stranger making me flustered under the cold cotton sheets.

'Michael.'

'I'm here.'

My hands flew to my head and I realised I was not wearing my head scarf.

'Get out of here!'

It came out louder than I intended and he looked taken aback.

'I'm sorry, I didn't mean to upset you.' He started to back away, but before he left he turned for a second and said, 'I know how this feels.'

I think I fell asleep again. I couldn't remember what it was like to control when and how I sleep. Something so simple that people take for granted and there I was, one minute thinking and talking, the next fast asleep.

As I opened my eyes it had become dark outside once more and I actually felt (just a tiny bit) better. I felt rested and although my head was still tender and sore, it was not the same pain that made me want to jump from a twelfth-storey window. The painkillers dolefully handed out that morning had offered a welcome reprieve.

In the absence of pain, my first thought was of Michael. God, I'd been rude. Maybe it would have been nice to talk to him for a while.

I realized I had never spoken to another young person who'd had chemo or cancer. Only elderly people, where although it was still cruel and unjust that they were being slowly taken by an illness, people would at least be able to say, 'Well, he had a good innings,' or 'He didn't want to fight any more, he lived a long and happy life, that's all that mattered.' Their funerals would be celebrations of a life filled with love and family, who would tell funny stories of the good old days with a drink in their hand and a tear in their eye.

No one would say that for the young victims. We were meant to be just getting started; we should have had our whole lives ahead of us. No cares in the world until at least our mid-thirties, when we might consider coming home at a reasonable hour, contemplate the thought of marrying the person we share a flat with, hear the tick of the biological clock (or at the very least, get a dog).

It seemed suddenly important that I speak to Michael and apologise. I might have been too self-absorbed to stop myself being incredibly rude to a stranger, but not all strangers have mesmerizingly intense eyes, and no one has ever unnerved me so pleasantly before.

I got up, without too much difficulty I was delighted to realise, and headed for the bathroom to splash water over my face. I got the fright of my life seeing Gollum staring back at me. (Since Dr Braby had made me over I'd asked Isabel to replace the mirror.)

Undeterred, I reached for the Ted Baker bag and repeated her magic as best as I could. I even applied some lip gloss and by the time I fastened the headscarf the way she taught me, I felt a little like Anna again.

A clean pair of white linen pyjamas plus a baby blue ballet cardigan and I was ready to try and make a new friend. I was so used to trailing up and down the corridor with a drip stand attached to me it felt strange to be leaving it behind. But there it was, redundant and lonely in the corner of the room.

I did not have to look very far for Michael because he was sitting on the bed in the side room opposite mine. He was wearing a beige cowboy hat and playing a guitar. Perhaps I was still dreaming.

***

I tap quietly on the door. 'Hello?'

He looks up at me and before he looks quickly away again, I catch it in his eyes. He is pleased to see me.

'Hi.' He shrugs casually.

'I wanted to say I'm sorry for shouting. I'm not quite myself these days. Well, I can be a bit moody but honestly, I don't normally bite strangers' heads off like that. But you said you know what it feels like so I just thought ...' I feel I'm rambling and my voice starts to trail off. I don't have a blonde mane to flick flirtatiously over my shoulder as I usually would and I feel somewhat at a loss. 'So ... sorry,' I turn to go but his voice stops me.

'It's OK, I do know. I've heard you yelling at most of your visitors these last few weeks. I should've been more prepared.'

I look at him, horrified, until he starts smiling. I reach out my hand to him.

'I'm Anna.'

'Michael.'

He tries to shake my outstretched hand but his IV won't pull that far. I step awkwardly round his things and find myself plonked in his visitors' chair – How forward. We finally shake hands.

We talk for a little while. I find out he likes country music, that he had been born in America and now runs an American-style riding centre north of Northampton with his father. He likes everything to do with being outdoors and has a dog called Lincoln. (I naturally wonder if he has a thirty-something wife.) I tell him I like dogs and horses, which is true, but I neglect to mention the fact I hate doing anything with my spare time other than lazing around with Jules watching trashy television shows. We had barely left the house at weekends since she'd had Sky installed, unless a Saturday night out beckoned and we recorded everything for a further laze fest on the Sunday.

I do not want him judging me for some reason. I am not normally one to care a great deal for what people think of me and could often be found boasting about the weekend we watched thirty-four back-to-back episodes of *Geordie Shore*. I want Michael to think I have more depth. He does look a little older than me; it is quite hard to tell because this illness (I'm sick of the C word) makes everyone look so much older. I wouldn't lie to him exactly, but if he asks how I spend my spare time I will have to think of something more worthwhile than endless parties and duvet days.

'How long did you live in America?' I ask, feeling it might be better to keep the spotlight over there for now.

'Like I say, I was born there, but my mom left when I was young.' He pauses for a second and looks down at his hands. 'She left after my little brother died and my dad raised me alone.'

'I'm so sorry, Michael.'

I want to put my hand over his, but he moves them before I have the chance and the moment passes.

'We had our own riding centre where tourists would come out and ride round Western-style. A taste of being a cowboy, they loved it.'

'So you had a Dude Ranch, that's so cool.'

He looks impressed. 'Exactly, a Dude Ranch. Anyway, a few years later one of the tourists caught Pops' eye and they fell in love. My stepmom, Caroline, didn't want to leave her family in England so we sold up and moved over here. I was only ten and we didn't have much family to leave behind, so we set up the business and it's been doing pretty good since. They got married nearly ten years ago and spend most of the time travelling; they wanted to retire, so I was running things; ready to take over 'til I got sick.'

It is the first time either of us has mentioned being ill, and it hangs in the air between us. I'm not ready for it yet. I love listening to him; he is so open and confident. Maybe I do worry too much about what other people think, but I am terrified he will find me transparent and boring while I find him so original. Let's face facts, I do not exactly have my looks to fall back on.

'So you're, like, twenty?'

'Nineteen. And you?'

'I might look a hundred and eight but I'm actually seventeen. And a half,' I add quickly, in case he thinks I am too young. 'Seventeen and a half.'

He smiles but it's more like a little laugh and he starts strumming on the guitar in his hands, singing jauntily '*She might look one hundred but she's only seventeen.*'

'And a half!' I try to say crossly, but I'm laughing too.

The night goes on like that, we laugh and share stories and I thank God I feel OK. I'm not rushing to the bathroom to throw up every five minutes. I just feel young and happy for the first time in a long time.

'Your scarf looks pretty.'

I blush furiously, feeling horribly self-conscious. 'Two months ago I had blonde hair.'

'Like a Palomino.' He's doing that half-smile, half-laugh thing again. It makes me disintegrate.

'What's a Palomino?' I ask him, holding his gaze.

'I might tell you one day.'

I smile at Michael, delighted at the thought that we might have another day, but I can see he suddenly looks tired.

'Are you OK?' I ask, and help him set his guitar down so he can lie back on the bed.

'I will be. They came round this morning and said the treatment's worked. I felt like that alone would kill me but the tumour's small enough to remove.'

'Where is it?'

'At the bottom of my back, near my spine. A dangerous place and it was too risky to operate, but now I'm all set for Wednesday. Prospects look good considering a while ago they thought I might not be able to walk again.'

He catches the look of fear that flickers across my face for only a second.

'Anna.'

'Michael, I'm happy you're going to be OK, I really am. But I should go. It's getting late and Nurse Ratched will have a ding dong if she finds me in here.' I mimic her raspy voice, '"Visiting hours are eleven 'til one, and six 'til eight. Not a minute before or after. Patients need rest."' I wagged my finger at him. '"Rest. Rest. Rest."'

'Anna,' he says gently.

I shrug and wrap my ballet cardy tightly around me, self-conscious once more. 'My chemo didn't work. They have to operate anyway, but it'll be a much higher risk. They never really put you in the picture properly but I forced them to. The tumour is growing too fast for the chemo to touch. It will, without a doubt, kill me very soon, so they may as well have a go at the operation. I'm going home to rest for a few weeks then I'll be back to face the music. I suppose I'm really going home to spend some quality time with the people I love before I die. It's got to beat living the rest of my life in this place, I guess. Mr Raj is trying to keep me positive, and even though I'm definitely quite stupid, I'm not stupid enough to believe he can pull it off and my life will go back to normal.'

***

There. I'd said it. I had told another person that I knew I was going to die. I had known it from the day I sat in the Alice in Wonderland chair and the black cloud appeared to loom patiently above me.

It felt good to share with him, but it pretty much put an end to any romantic thoughts I may have had. Before, we were simply Michael and Anna, holding one another's gaze for beautiful drawn-out moments. Now he was just another patient, except he would get better and I wouldn't.

'Come here.'

He moves across the bed and holds his arms out to me. It feels like the most natural thing in the world to lie down beside him. This man I have known for a few hours holds me in his arms and tells me everything will be OK. And d'you know something? For the next hour and half everything is perfectly fine.

Sometime later I wake in my own bed, having crept back across the corridor in the very early hours of the morning; I can hear the nurses chatting quietly at the night station but no one seems to have noticed me. I still have butterflies in my stomach. Michael has changed everything, and all I can think of is him.

Does your mind ever race ahead of itself and create scenarios for the future? I had envisaged a thousand different roles. How we will *both* overcome our illnesses and spend our lives together riding horses and wearing cowboy hats.

Now the early morning light is creeping through my side room window, I am beginning to have my doubts. I feel sick again – Emotionally and physically drained. I reach for my diary and see it is Sunday already. I am going home in a little over a week.

So how can anything ever happen for us? We will be miles apart. Michael will recover from his operation and I have yet to face mine. I am truly disheartened and manage to convince myself that he will not care either way; he will focus on getting well again and finding a girlfriend with hair. I find this more depressing than my current life expectancy.

I close my eyes and relax my mind until I consciously will myself to fall asleep. It isn't too hard, I don't feel I have much to stay awake for. Maybe I imagined this connection with Michael to distract myself from the awful things I should have been trying to face. I have to contemplate what is left of my life, concentrate on how things should be handled with my family. Here I am thinking of how it will feel to be with a man I barely know, when something deep down tells me I am probably the farthest thing from his mind.

At least I have been honest, I think sadly. He can feel free to feel sorry for the poor girl he shared a few hours with once. I can see him in the pub with his friends in years to come, telling them about the girl in the room opposite his who didn't make it. They tell him he was one of the lucky ones and he smiles and goes back to chatting up the barmaid.

A nurse with those damn stomach injections brings me round again, but she looks really young and nervous so I don't shout at her. I even nearly smile a little.

'Sorry, Anna,' she says. 'I'm Rebecca. This is to help prevent blood clots when you're lying down so much. They told me to try and let you sleep.'

'Did *they* say I was scary?'

She just laughs. 'I'd shout at people too if they kept coming at me with needles.'

'Have I had any visitors?' I try to sound casual.

'Yes, your mum and sister were here at little while ago, but you were fast asleep so they're coming back in an hour.'

'No-one else?'

'I don't think so. Were you expecting somebody?'

'Not really, I just sleep so much I barely know where I am or who's been to see me.'

She picked up my headscarf from where it had fallen by the bed.

'You like horses then?'

I must have looked confused because she pointed to the scarf again. 'Horseshoes, and the picture by your bed.'

I look to where she is pointing and my eyes fall on a picture of a pale blonde horse, with a flowing mane that shines like 24-carat gold, propped against my bedside lamp. I try to contain myself until she's left the room, then fall off the bed in my haste to reach it. The picture shows an orangey red sky and a majestic horse reared defiantly up towards it, as though she knows even the sunset cannot compete against her beauty. It is called 'The Palomino'. I look at it for a few moments then turn the card.

Meet me in Day Room One when you wake up, my beautiful Anna.
    X

That is the moment I fall in love with Michael Torino.

***

We spent what was left of Sunday (six hours and forty-five minutes) sitting alone together in the day room – And every day for the next eight days. We talked about our childhoods. Though he didn't want to talk much about his brother, he did say he was called Benjamin, or Benji.

'I think he hated being called Benji, but it sort of stuck.'

He paused and took a sip of water.

'What's your sister like?'

He was nearly an expert subject changer as me.

'Is she as charming as you?' He gave the little laugh again.

'Isabel is far more charming than I am and she hates her real name too. Everyone calls her Izzy.' I look up and see two people walking towards us. 'Actually, judge for yourself.'

As Isabel walked in with my mother, my heart crashed to the floor. She looked gorgeous in her irritatingly understated manner and much older than her almost fourteen years. She wore skinny jeans, ballet pumps and a T-shirt that shows off her slender brown arms and an unintentional touch of bare midriff. Her chestnut hair was tied back in a tight ponytail (I knew she was being sensitive because she *never* wears her hair up – it's always cascading down her back and over her shoulders like mine used to be.) For weeks I've seen nothing but this damn ponytail and it annoyed the hell out of me. Maybe I want as many reasons for anger as possible, and her trying to take some of them away from me is making things worse. I forgot about trying to be nice in front of Michael and snapped at her.

'That's my T-shirt. It's far too small for you.'

Izzy was having none of it. She ignored me and held her hand out to Michael.

'So you're the reason she's cheered up.'

He started to laugh as he shook her hand but stopped abruptly when he saw my fuming face.

'Well, you do have a reputation on the ward as a bit of a grump, darling.'

Darling. He called me darling like we had been married for twenty-five years. The sky was blue again and for all I cared, Izzy could have walked through the ward wearing nothing but nipple tassels.

'This is Michael,' I say ever so sweetly, 'and this is *Isabel*, my sister, and Lilly, my mother.'

'Lillian,' she corrected, looking horrified, to my greatest satisfaction. My grandparents had been nineteen when they found out they were expecting. At that time they lived in a caravan as part of a travelling community. Lillian was born a blonde-haired little angel and they doted on her. For years, they told us the story of how they found her under a lily pad when she was a tiny baby and decided to bring her home. My mother cringes whenever she hears it. I suppose it suited her when she was little, wearing only a smile and daisy chain. Now she dresses in Jaeger and Donna Karan, and the smile has been replaced with a dissatisfied frown.

'Nice to meet you both.' Michael was oblivious to the chip on her shoulder pad.

'How are you? They say you can come home soon.' Izzy looked at me warily, prepared for another attack. My mood swings have become so erratic and she looked quite scared.

'I feel OK, apart from the headaches and knocking over or dropping everything I touch.'

There was an awkward silence which Michael took as his cue to leave.

'I'll come see you after visiting hours; I'll get some chocolate from the canteen.'

He kissed my hand like it was the most natural thing in the world and I couldn't help smiling as he left the three of us alone.

'God, he's gorgeous, Anna!'

My smile disappeared and I glared daggers at Izzy.

'Oh, great sis, fancy him, do you? I'm sure you'll get your claws into him when I'm dead.'

I spat out the last word and she looked close to crying, but straightened her shoulders and said with perhaps more conviction than she felt, 'Stop. Stop pushing everyone away. This is hard for us too, you know.'

I snorted derisively, doubting she would want to swap places. My sister and silent mother seemed to have sucked what little life was left out of the room. Or maybe it had just left with Michael.

'Do you think I want the two of you staring at me with cow eyes? Full of pity! I can't stand it any more. Please, just leave me alone.' I looked up at my sister through streaming tears and saw the flush of colour in her cheeks where mine were now gaunt and sallow. Her hair is thick and shiny, full of the life I am losing. Looking at her just reminded me that the harder I tried to hold on, the faster I seemed to be falling.

Mum reached towards me with such utter uncertainty that I lost control once again. Why did she find it so hard to comfort me? What had I ever done to feel this alone?

'Get away from me!' I yelled. My face and neck were wet with tears. I tried to throw Isabel off but she was too strong now and wrapped her arms around me so I couldn't move. As we sat in the same chair rocking and crying together, I glanced up for a second to see my mother's back as she left the room, and I grabbed on to Izzy as though my life depended on it.

***

About an hour later we are still squashed in the same recliner, but now we have acquired a blanket and a cup of sweet tea each from a concerned auxiliary nurse. I even manage to share a KitKat with Iz for the pleasure and normality of dunking it into our tea like we used to.

'Do you remember that time you fell off Starlight?' she asks.

I nod against her shoulder.

We had been riding in the meadow and I was showing off as usual, trying to get Star to jump a fallen log. I cantered her determinedly up to it but instead of jumping, she stuck her hooves in the ground suddenly and I flew over her head. When you fall from a height like that, you don't feel yourself going down; it is more like the ground is coming up – and at an alarmingly fast rate. Recently, I have found the simplest of things difficult to recall, but I can see that bumpy ground coming towards me like it was yesterday. Afterwards there was nothing until I opened my eyes to see my mother beside me in the meadow as Izzy had run to get her. *She* was crying. Why was she the one crying when I had been the human catapult? Mother kept asking over and over was I all right and what on earth had I been thinking, and I recall closing my eyes to try and shut her out.

A doctor visited a little while later and said I would be fine, that I just had a very mild concussion and that Lillian should keep an eye on me for the next few hours.

Izzy had tried to cheer me up by doing impressions of what I had looked like flying through the air, and while I laughed uproariously as she flung herself off the settee, she proceeded to bang her head on the coffee table, which of course ended up being my fault as well.

When Father walked in we were watching cartoons with matching egg-shaped bumps on our foreheads. He gave us a little iced bun each he'd brought back from the deli and planted a kiss on our noses, making us laugh again – he always would kiss our forehead, but wanted to avoid the two bruised bumps.

Dad was furious with our mother, and we looked at each other with widened eyes as he asked her to go upstairs so they could 'Discuss this privately.'

I heard a lot of banging and imagined her throwing things and shouting. My father never lost his temper so I knew it was her – Always making things miserable.

'I don't remember Dad even being there,' says Izzy, as I remember his annoyance that our mother hadn't taken better care of us. 'I hardly remember him at all. He was always working when we were little. I just remember Mum.'

'Yes, working all hours because she was spending his money on that stupid bloody house. It's not even a home, it's like a museum.'

'Not our special room though, that was always a tip! God, I haven't been up there for years, not since we left primary school.'

The room Izzy is talking about is the attic which Mother had converted into a playroom for us when we were young. It was full of toys and a rocking horse, and it was certainly very pretty with its flowery wallpaper. But what no one, certainly not Izzy, remembers is that the mother she tries to defend used to lock us in that beautiful room and leave us there.

***

Michael came to my room a little while later, with chocolate as promised. I eyed the Twix nervously, as the half a KitKat I'd eaten earlier was like an eight-course banquet these days. I didn't want to seem ungrateful but I didn't want to throw up in front of him either. So I nibbled the piece he gave me and sighed gratefully as he bit into the second biscuit himself.

'I came back ages ago but you and your sister looked like you needed to be alone.'

He looked a little concerned, so I smile bravely and told him, 'Thank you. Izzy always makes me feel better. I mean she drives me around the bend and back, but, you know ...'

'You love her?'

I shrug, a little embarrassed as I am not exactly in touch with my emotional side.

'Yes, I do,' I replied. Then, just in case he thought he might love her also, I added, 'When she's not being immature she's OK, I suppose. Bit childish, really. She still picks her nose.'

Michael did his funny half laugh and I felt like

he was laughing at me, so I nibbled at the Twix a little more seductively. I considered fluttering my eyelashes before I remembered I had none.

My old friend self-doubt stopped by for a visit, and I started to wonder why he was being so nice to me. He knew I was a goner, did he just feel sorry for me? I can't stand being pitied, so I pushed the thought away with a more comforting replacement. 'Of course!' I told myself. 'He just wants to have sex with me. He has a thing for invalids because we are desperate and needy. He thinks I will be so grateful for some attention in my current state that he can just push me on the bed and have his way with me!'

God, if only. Until now he had been a perfect gentleman, possibly because a matter of days ago he had undergone an eight-hour surgery to remove the tumour by his spine. I'd spent as much time in his room while he was in recovery as possible. And during those simple days, I had started to feel a little better too.

In my determination to make Michael eat, I sat an example by making the effort myself, and even Mr Raj said I had a little colour in my cheeks. He said this with a twinkle in his eye, and I think most of the staff thought that the chance of love blossoming on the oncology ward was a welcome if surprising occurrence.

Not that they had dared to say so. My mood swings were still unpredictable, although looking after Michael, however briefly, made me forget my own plight for a while. One night I kissed his forehead and actually went back to my own room smiling. I was walking on air and if anyone had seen me sailing through ward five in the silent hours before dawn they would have thought I'd change places with no one.

So feelings were certainly growing between us. Yet here he was, sitting a respectable distance away from me in his wheelchair, absentmindedly eating half a Twix. I hoped he was secretly wondering what colour my underwear was.

He may have read my mind as I blushed and he smiled at me again. 'So, this is weird.'

'What is?' My heart was beating suddenly fast.

'Well, you know.' He looked a little awkward. 'We haven't exactly met in the usual circumstances. We're both ill and stuck in this place ... and you're leaving tomorrow. I like you so much, Anna. I don't want this to be the last time we see each other.'

It would have taken me days, perhaps weeks, to think of a way to say those same words to Michael. He just said what he thought, and I wished I could be like that instead of considering all angles: whether or not opening up would work in my favour, or if I'd be rejected. I followed his lead instead.

'I like you too – A lot, actually. It just feels doomed; beginnings should be movie dates and romantic strolls, not brain tumours and imminent death.'

'I saw your mum in the canteen,' he said eagerly. 'She said you can get through this. In fact, she's sure that you will. I really like her, Anna; she has such a good way of looking at things and cares about you so much.'

I said the next words very slowly, as though I couldn't quite believe them. 'You've been talking to my mother?'

He missed my tone and carried on, blissfully unaware of the tornado picking up ferocious momentum.

'Yes, we had a coffee while you and Izzy were talking. She looked very upset so I joined her and we had a really nice conversation. She told me about you when you were little, how strong-minded you are. She's so sure you'll get through this it really inspired me. After what you told me I thought there was no hope, but Lillian says Mr Raj is brilliant ... and perhaps you were being a bit pessimistic about your prognosis.'

His voice trailed off uncertainly as he saw the look on my face. Michael looked distinctly worried.

'So you both think I'm lying?' I gave a laugh that sounded very ugly. 'Mother of the Year is telling everyone her daughter is exaggerating her illness. Did she tell you about the time I used her red lipstick to dot my face with chicken pox because I didn't want to be in the nativity play? Or when I feigned feeling sick to avoid a family day out? This is priceless! Now she's telling everyone I'm pretending to have a brain tumour. Look!'

I pulled off the headscarf I had so carefully placed earlier that day.

'I've even shaved my hair off to go along with the charade! This is how it all started, you know – Me not wanting to go to sixth form, being sent to a real doctor. It was all an elaborate ploy!'

I was absorbed in my rage. How could she try and turn Michael against me? I hadn't noticed him reach for me, and when I looked up his face is so close to mine I can see the grey flecks in his eyes.

'No!' He sounded distraught but I no longer cared. My dream was spoiled and sullied. 'Anna, please, it was nothing like that. Of course she knows how dangerous it is, she believes you're a fighter, that you're stronger than she's ever been. She has to believe you'll be OK because she can't face the alternative – Like I can't.'

I could barely hear him as I shook with rage. I reached past him and pressed for the nurse. 'I have a terrible headache,' I said coldly and with a calmness I didn't feel. 'Please leave me alone. Despite what my mother has told you I *am* too ill to deal with all of this. So what if we like each other? I just want to get out of here tomorrow and forget about this place, that's all I can think about right now.'

'Do you want to forget about me?'

I met his eyes and my heart dissolved like ice in fire.

'Yes, Michael. That is exactly what I want.'

***

When the nurse arrives, I grossly exaggerate the extent of my headache. I have done that a few times in here because the drugs are so good. A few excruciating minutes after swallowing the little capsules and I am drifting away on a euphoric cloud. The razor-sharp pain in my chest that told me I had blown it with Michael ebbs away as I fall deeper under the sedative spell. I am anaesthetized once more, not by wine or Father's port, but by some pills I can't pronounce the name of but have every intention of becoming very familiar with.

I wake up with a dry mouth and a cloudy head. Mother is packing my things and I can hear Izzy saying, 'She's waking up, I think. God, what did they give her?'

I open my eyes another painful crack and see her concerned face. She pulls me up to a sitting position and holds some juice with a straw to my lips. I ask her where my father is, the same question I have asked every day since he last visited.

'He's still in New Zealand.' The voice of doom from Lillian, who must love to be the bearer of bad news. 'He decided to stay out there and finish his appraisal when he found out you were being sent home. You'll see him on Sunday.'

'I knew he'd be back soon,' I say smugly, and she makes a noise I cannot quite decipher. She is holding the palomino picture Michael gave me and I snatch it from her.

'I was going to put it in your suitcase, Anna. We need to get going; you were discharged hours ago.'

I swing myself stiffly from the bed and try to walk with nonchalance to the bathroom. But my head is spinning and as I wobble Izzy looks away quickly. She knows when to offer help and when to let me get on with it.

I let them sort out my room and sit on the bathroom floor with the door closed. Silent tears flow as I remember the way I treated Michael. It was hardly his fault that my mother was evil and wanted everyone to hate me as much as she did. I was still holding the picture he had left me, what seemed like eons ago. Under his original note was a number that hadn't been there before, and I realized he must have come back to my room while I was sleeping. I took a moment to cringe a little. I've never been the prettiest of sleepers, so Lord knows what I must've looked like last night – Red, puffy eyes from crying, possibly drooling, and comatose with knock-out painkillers. Still, he had given me his mobile number and written in very small letters under it, 'Don't just leave me.'

I smile sadly and think of what could have been.

How my heart had soared when he asked me to meet him in the day room and called me 'beautiful'. I could never imagine feeling like that again. There was no room in my new world for such happiness, it just didn't fit in with everything I was about to face up to: Like painting a rainbow on a torture chamber's wall.

I allow myself one last look before tearing the golden horse into tiny pieces.

CHAPTER FIVE

ELM TREE

I spend the journey home dosing in and out of consciousness, and it's not until I open my eyes that I see we are not headed for Northampton, but winding through the familiar country roads to Elm Tree House. I glance sideways at my mother and notice her knuckles go white as she grips the steering wheel. She knows what's coming and I do not intend to disappoint her.

'Please tell me we're not going home. Please tell me you haven't completely lost the plot and are taking me back to the museum.'

Silence.

I spin round to face Izzy, who looks like a mouse in front of an angry viper. 'We had no choice, Anna. Gramps has flu and the doctor said absolutely not. You can't be around sick people.'

I digest this in seconds and grab on to my next

thought. 'Take me to Jules!' Jules and her boyfriend Eddie shared a grim flat in an equally grim location, but anywhere was preferable to what had been proposed.

'With Jules and Eddie? Do you really think they'll take care of you? They've only visited a couple of times; they have no clue what type of care you need.'

That silences me for a second. It is true that my visitors seem to have declined in line with my hair follicles. The sicker I looked, the less they came.

'Izzy, please, don't make me spend my last few weeks with *her* looking after me. It will be the actual death of me.'

I groan dramatically but I do feel utterly doomed.

My one chink of light had been the warm, relaxed home of my grandparents. They would have left me alone to wallow in my misery, and turned a blind eye if I raided the drinks cabinet. Now I would be offered endless cups of green tea and miracle cures from *her* herbal remedies collection. She'd tell me to stop feeling sorry for myself, and I could already feel the sun pierce my eyes as she pulled open the drapes at some ungodly hour every morning.

Izzy knows I am upset and leans forward from the back seat to put her arms around me. 'I'll be there. I'll be there to look after you. It's better this way, trust me, Anna.' She leans forward and whispers in my ear, 'I'll sneak you in the odd brandy and Coke.'

I smile and lean my head against hers.

***

Despite my gloom at the change of plans for my 'rest' period, my heart lifts just a little as we pull on to the long driveway that leads to Elm Tree. Tudor-style with white walls and black beams, it's actually quite beautiful. Surrounding the house are green lawns, lily ponds and weeping willows that wouldn't be out of place in a Monet. Despite having a regular gardener, the grounds had been left a while so wild flowers could flourish, and poppies surround the low stone walls. Perhaps my father had had his say outside, because inside was one hundred per cent Mother.

This becomes all too depressingly apparent as we open the huge front door to the entrance hall that looked more hotel than home: Mahogany furniture, a round table supporting an oversized Japanese vase of faux flowers and a burgundy Chesterfield. Hardwood flooring made our arrival echo around the walls, as the house came out of its high-polished silence. The familiar smell of air freshener and cleaning products filled my nostrils, and I felt sick.

'Here we are,' Lillian says quietly. 'Do you want to go to go to your bedroom or shall I make up the living room?'

I scowl at her. I'm still angry with her for talking to Michael. Not that I would give her the satisfaction of saying so.

'Why not shove me in the attic, Mummy dearest? That way you won't have to follow me round with disinfectant everywhere I go.'

I'm very satisfied to see her knocked down by my words, and head for the drawing room, intentionally choosing the one room she would not want me ensconced. It was specifically reserved for entertaining Father's important guests before dinner. We had never been allowed in there – it was mostly white. Sofas, carpets, even the walls were ghostly alabaster. I open the door, leaving Izzy and Mother whispering something at each other, and take in the antiques and exquisite paintings. But the room is cold and unwelcoming; I have to force myself across the threshold.

Above the fireplace is a painting of three angels reaching down to a cherub offering gifts of golden musical instruments. Rows of portraits hang under brass display lamps on each wall. People from a different century, who once sat for those paintings with beating hearts, had now been a long time dead. Ten pairs of cold, unsmiling eyes watch me as I step tentatively backwards and out of the room.

'What a shithole,' I say loudly, making my mother wince. 'I'll go straight to *my* room. No doubt you've taken my absence as an excuse to tidy up and snoop around.'

I turn the brass knob and push the door open, its drag familiar over the thick pile carpet, and I see my room is just as I left it. She has made the bed, but that is all. My green dress is still on the floor next to the open wardrobe, drawers hang off their hinges where I dragged my clothes out in haste. The pictures of horses I have outgrown but never want to take down remain Blu-tacked to the walls. I am so taken aback she has not gone through it all that I jump when I heard her voice next to me.

'I like a little chaos, Anna. When you were in hospital I would come to this room and be comforted.' She pauses and does the little cough she does when she feels awkward. 'We've missed you terribly these last few weeks. Just waking up here, having breakfast together ...'

***

We had argued the day I went into hospital, but there was nothing new there. I told her it was all her fault that Dad worked away so much, that he couldn't stand her and neither could I.

I was about to say she could have at least tidied up for today when she knew I would be back, and did she expect me to do chores already? But something stopped me and I just mumbled, 'Thanks.' Her cold hand touched my arm and I unintentionally flinched, spoiling the moment.

On cue, Izzy breezed in and busied herself by picking up my dress and closing the drawers.

'I'll start dinner,' Mum said, bidding a hasty retreat leaving Izzy and me alone.

'What now?' I said, feeling lost.

She looked serious for a second, then beamed and said, 'Let's try on all of your jeans and see if they aren't too big for you.'

'Ooh you're a genius, Isabel!'

I ran to hug her then started pulling my clothes out of the wardrobe.

To my absolute glee, the jeans that I had once shoe-horned myself into now slipped easily over my slim thighs and hung loosely round my waist. Izzy even indulged my euphoria and tried on the same pair to show me how much fatter she was in comparison. We screamed with laughter as she lay on the bed and I stood over her, pulling furiously at the zip until it popped.

All the fun and exertion soon took its toll on me, and I climbed under the covers half an hour later despite her ardent protesting.

'Come have dinner first,' Izzy pleaded. 'Mum's gone to a lot of trouble.'

I rolled my eyes and said I'd have a Pot Noodle later, then waited until Izzy left the room before I pulled my bag onto my lap and reached for the painkillers I had insisted to Mr Raj that I needed.

I could not simply lie there waiting for sleep.

My thoughts would turn to Michael and the pain of losing him. I swallowed two, then another for good measure, and welcomed oblivion.

***

The next few days passed in something of a blur, but I remember spending a lot of time in bed. I would open my eyes at various intervals and see my sister's concerned face, tell her to get lost, and she would agree to leave me alone if I just had a sip of this or a bite of that. I suppose they thought I was asleep one afternoon when I overheard their conversation regarding my lack of energy.

'Did you speak to him?'

'Yes, darling. He sounded surprised she was spending so much time in bed because the week before coming home she had significantly more energy.'

'When she was looking after Michael...' Izzy sounds worried. 'I don't know what happened and I'm too scared to talk to her about it. I asked her yesterday if she'd heard from him and she threw a protein shake at me.'

'Well, we can't focus on that now. We need to get her up and about. Maybe some fresh air or proper food will help. I'm trying, Izzy. I've been cooking food that will do her good. It's not my forte but Lord knows I've tried.'

'I know, Mum. We'll give her half an hour then wake her up. At least she'll be in a better mood when she hears that Father's coming home today.'

I shot up out of my pretend sleep like a corpse springing up from its coffin, giving them both the fright of their lives. 'When? When is he coming home?'

My father had been in New Zealand since before I was diagnosed. I needed to get straightened out before he saw me. A pang of fear washed over me. He would get such a shock when he saw his 'used to be so pretty' little girl.

'Oh, so you are awake.' Izzy looked cross but a little bit relieved. 'I'll help you get ready.'

I washed my face and sprayed on some deodorant, before letting Izzy do my make-up and pencil on some dark blonde eyebrows. She is the only one who seems to do this properly. I've taken to screaming 'eyebrows!' at the top of my voice if I need them done and she's not in the immediate vicinity.

'God, Anna,' she'd said last week. 'What must the staff think? I could hear you in the lift!'

'Hurry up!' I'd giggled. 'I'm seeing Michael soon. I need my brows.'

A lifetime ago.

'Why are your hands shaking?' she now asked, as she carefully stencilled over the original arch above my eyes.

'Because I have a brain tumour,' I replied bluntly, reaching for my trusty pills as I felt my anxiety awaken when I thought about Michael.

'They didn't used to, that wasn't one of your symptoms.' Now she looked nervous. 'Mum talked to Mr Raj earlier.' She felt me stiffen but carried on bravely. 'He says those painkillers you're taking are only for emergencies; when you really can't bear a headache. He said if you take too many they'll make you feel very tired and depressed. He said they might even make your headaches worse in the end. So, err, perhaps you should cut back on them a bit?'

I looked at her defiantly and popped another two. 'Mother of the Year has been talking to Mr Raj behind my back. Again. What a surprise. For your information, these tablets are the only things keeping me from wringing the woman's neck.'

She finished my make-up in silence and I did not bother to thank her as I walked unsteadily from the room, holding tightly to the bannister as I descended the stairs.

***

My father did not show up until the following day. He said the traffic was so bad he had stayed overnight at a Traveller's Inn. He listened patiently as I sobbed my heart out, and my pleasure at seeing him had been completely ruined by the fact my mother failed to wake me earlier. I woke up to see him sitting by my bed, looking horrified.

'I tried to wake you several times,' she said, but I in no way believed her. I knew she was jealous that I loved him dearly, but I could hardly believe she would have been so spiteful. You see, my father is terrified of sick people. He never talks about weakness or ill health, he thinks everyone should just be civilized and get on with things. Even when my mother was pregnant with Izzy, I heard Grandma tell Gramps how he was 'repulsed' at her growing belly and the concept of childbirth. So it was all the more important for me to be up and dressed and looking the best I could – I didn't want to make him feel uncomfortable, which, right now, he inevitably did.

'Couldn't you have got her some sort of wig?' Even I was slightly taken aback at his tone, but instead of explaining how I hated the feel of them and that I was scared of looking ridiculous, my mother turned on her heel and left the room.

'It's OK, Annabel,' he said, handing me a linen handkerchief to indicate the tears could stop now. 'I'll have Leona find one for you.' Leona was his personal assistant and in charge of our birthday and Christmas presents if Father was working away. 'The very best!' He sounded so triumphant that I neglected to mention I had screamed and spat in my mother's face the day she brought a selection of wigs into the hospital for me.

'Thanks, Daddy. I need to freshen up, I'll see you downstairs.'

After he leaves, their shouting in the kitchen finds its familiar path through the echoing walls of

Elm Tree to my bedroom. I couldn't hear everything, but I did make out something about her being bloody useless. Too right.

***

With my new, rather chic, pale blonde wig and Izzy's eyebrow magic, I critique my latest reflection a little less harshly. The wig is from a London boutique, made of real hair, and my father even paid a stylist to come to our house and cut it for me. It now frames my face with a sweeping fringe and layers flow down past my shoulders. I tell Izzy as often as possible that I no longer have split ends, and what a shame she does.

I declined Father's offer to take me to London to have it cut at a salon. The tablets I rely on really do make me tired, although lately I have started to take even more as they do not seem to be working as quickly. I shake less, though, and am even steadier on my feet. So much for taking too many – I felt better!

So it is with relieved expressions that Jules and Eddie see me walk into the living room. This is their first visit since I left hospital and I note they have found Father's wine rack.

We all hug a bit awkwardly and sit down on the deep set sofas. I am much brighter and though I still feel that someone has ripped my heart out and stuck it in a blender, I push Michael to the back of my mind and smile at my friends.

'You look fine to me!' Eddie says after knocking back his first glass of wine. 'You really are a big faker, Anna Winters. Obviously nothing the bloody matter with you!'

Jules is also topping her glass up and I have only taken two sips. Alcohol has lost its appeal lately, so while I appreciate Eddie's good humour, that alone tells me I'm not at all well.

'You do look great, hun,' Jules tells me, drinking Father's Châteauneuf-du-Pape as though it were Vimto. 'We were really worried about you after the hospital visit. I mean, you could have warned us!'

Her laugh is a bit hollow and I take a few more sips of wine, feeling vulnerable. I look over my shoulder and see the brass bell I had found in Father's office. It started off as a joke but I'd taken to ringing it quite frequently for Izzy. She appears seconds later and Jules and Eddie start laughing, which breaks the tension, but only a little.

'What now, Anna?' Izzy looks very cross, which makes them laugh harder. 'I'm trying to do homework. I can't drop everything every time you want a cup of tea or your toenails painted!'

I secretly love it when Izzy gets so mad at me; it makes me feel less like an invalid and more like the bossy sister who has always driven her crazy.

'More wine.'

I lift the empty bottle and glare at her defiantly as she eyes the expensive label. As I stare at her, I try to tell my sister, just by my opening my eyes a little wider, that I am not comfortable and I need her.

She rolls her eyes dramatically, but I know she gets it as she returns a few minutes later with a slightly less expensive bottle and a juice for herself. She plonks herself next to me protectively and calls me a loser.

I feel better now she has joined us, and I tell her she is fat.

***

We drink wine until the afternoon descends into November twilight, and Eddie says they should go because he only has one headlight on his old Volkswagen Golf. He yawns dramatically and stands up. 'I need an early night, anyway, the neighbour's dog howls all night like a banshee.'

'Your neighbour doesn't have a dog.' I sound confused, remembering the mean-spirited drunk who lives in the rundown house next door to theirs – Hardly an animal-loving type.

'He does now,' Jules says, as she and Eddie look nervously at each other. 'Speaking of home, and I know this may not be the best time what with your, err …'

'Brain tumour?' I offer silently.

'… Illness and all that, but we've missed you coming round. So don't be a stranger, eh?'

A tiny part of me wondered if they missed me or

the bottles of booze I used to bring.

They both mumble their goodbyes and I hear Izzy telling them curtly that no, she couldn't lend them a few quid for petrol.

Izzy comes back in and says, 'Hope he gets done for drink driving. What a prick.'

I would have normally defended my friends, but I say nothing and let her cover me with a blanket while I fall asleep in front of the crackling fire.

***

I open my eyes to the dreaded smell of nut loaf. Since I have been home my mother's attempts at healthy cooking have become depressingly worse. My heart lifts a little when I remember that Father will be joining us, and I even manage to eat some crusty bread and butter while he smiles at me approvingly.

'Now then,' he says. 'You certainly look better than the sickly ragamuffin I came home to. I'm glad I came back when I did; at least you've got a fighting chance to beat this thing. You need all your strength for next week, when they try to remove the er ...'

'Cancer?' Another silent suggestion.

'... the problem. As it were.' He coughs, looking disappointed, and Mother intervenes quickly.

'Your room is a tip, Anna.' I'm surprised at her perceptiveness – she knows I prefer to be treated as normally as possible, so I indulge her and tell her to piss off.

A loud cough from Father, who does not understand why Mum and Isabel share a smile.

He witters on about work and says he really ought to be getting back across the pond soon, and I feel worse that it is my fault he is treading the eggshells of our new family life instead of doing the job he loves.

It surprises me to realize that things had been slightly better before he came home. I could not put my finger on it but there was less tension or something. I push the guilty thought to one side and reach for some fruit, winning another smile from the man I dote on.

***

As I lie in bed later that night, alone and in the dark, real fear washes over me. Have you ever been truly afraid? You'll never forget the feeling. Terror squeezing your heart in tight hands, your panicked response as your pulse quickens and you struggle to breathe. It comes for me now, and there is nowhere to hide.

What if I don't survive the operation? Somewhere inside me I sense a fantastical truth that I was not going to. Should I be enlightened by now to what life is really about and what we are doing here anyway?

I wish that a sense of peace would replace this

unending fear that I am going to fall into darkness. And so too will each of us until no one remembers my ever being here at all.

I want to run out into the night screaming, 'I'm here! I'm alive, I'm somebody good … I have a place in this world!'

And perhaps if I believed that, I would run out of Elm Tree and dance like a ghost through the meadow. I might stand some sort of chance against fate. Instead, I choose to stay in my familiar gloom, pulling the blankets more tightly around myself, wondering why those words would sound so empty and hollow.

Someone once told me we should forget whatever past we've been painting, that the future is a vast blank canvas rolling out in front of us. Empty, untouched, and waiting to be filled with the stories of our lives.

Now my canvas had been torn away in front of me. Before I had even begun to sketch outlines to fill its open spaces, it's ripped short, taking with it my future.

Do we have to be so close to death to appreciate life? If life is a journey, does there have to be an end?

As I count the days I have left, I hope that death is just a big lie. Perhaps we fall asleep in this world and wake up renewed in the next. Somewhere better, somewhere I belong.

I wish I had explored the world and grasped

hold of every opportunity life had thrown at me, run through every newly opened door with a sense of adventure – Believed in myself.

I cry silently into my blankets and wait for the pills to take effect. They don't. Not even my trusted cloud of oblivion will come for me tonight.

I wonder if I had taken better care of myself and not made so many foolish decisions, would I still be suffering such an illness? Was I being punished? I feel suddenly overwhelmed by an unpleasant memory of a year ago, one I had tried desperately to forget.

I lost my virginity on this bed.

***

My father was rarely at home. He worked away for months on end and Mother had gone out for the evening, dramatically assured that at sixteen I was more than capable of taking care of Izzy for a few hours. The moment she left I swore my sister to secrecy and summoned Daniel, the only boyfriend I'd ever had, to come over.

Despite finding Elm Tree stuffy and oppressive, I loved to see my friends' expressions as they saw where I lived. The house spoke of wealth and good taste; I would walk a little taller and pull my accent up a few notches as I showed them around.

'This is Father's study,' I had told Daniel grandly, smiling as his eyes widened at the treasures within. An enormous brass eagle commanded my father's mahogany desk, silently screeching at intruders.

'Can we go in?' he whispered, and I snorted with disdain.

'Of course we can go in! This is *my* home, Daniel. We can do what we like.'

I refrained from mentioning that the last time Izzy and I had ventured into the private study, Father all but skinned us alive. I swung my legs from his great leather recliner and Daniel tentatively raised the upper half of a huge ceramic globe to reveal the hidden alcohol cache beneath. It had been my turn to look surprised and he grinned at me devilishly. There was a challenging note to his voice that made me regret having been quite so smug. 'My uncle has one of these. Fancy a tipple?'

Daniel was in the year above me at school. I didn't particularly like him, but an older boyfriend granted much kudos amongst the girls in my clique and we were forever trying to out-do one another. Danny was older, played football, *and* smoked.

My heart had begun to pound and an uneasy feeling of guilt washed over me. I suddenly wished I had just watched movies and ate popcorn with Izzy like she had wanted to do, instead of sending her forlornly to her room. I had spent the last few years wishing to be older, to be a grown-up exactly in a scenario like this – with a good-looking boy looking hazily at me and offering me a drink.

This memory had been uncomfortably buried,

but it is so vivid now as I recall my first taste of whiskey, how it burned through me like fire down to the pit of my stomach. He had held my hand firmly as he led me upstairs and lay me on the bed and I obediently consented. Half curious, half petrified beyond imagining. This boy was a stranger to me. High school was just a soap opera to my girlfriends and I. We were only supposed to play the parts of the on-screen adults; holding hands down corridors, flicking our hair flirtatiously as we watched the boys kick a ball around, and rolling our eyes dramatically at one another as we complained of their latest antics.

My heart had pounded as he roughly tugged down my jeans and underwear in one pull, unzipping his fly, and offering me the occasional peck on the lips to show his gratitude. Panic gripped me, but I could not have stopped him. Rebecca Hartwood had done that last year and spent all of Year Eleven being called frigid. My mind felt numbed by the whiskey but there was no escaping the pain as he jabbed away between my legs. I didn't know what I was supposed to be feeling, but surely not this? He came with a surprised look on his face and although he never told me so, I had imagined this was his first time too. Neither of us knew what to do afterwards, and perhaps he could see I was close to tears, for he gave an empty laugh and told me to lighten up. 'We've been seeing each other for months, Anna.' Shrugging his shoulders, he pulled up his jeans, and shortly afterwards, left.

I can remember curling up into a ball, tenderly touching between my legs and seeing only a little blood on my cold fingertips. Not the gallons of gore Nancy Page in Year Twelve had led us to believe.

With mixed emotions, I had eventually risen and pulled on my pale pink pyjama bottoms, looking at my reflection as I splashed cold water onto my face. I looked the same. 'No big deal,' I told myself with a lot more nonchalance than I had felt at the time. 'At least I've *actually* done it now.' I was left slightly bewildered what all the pandemonium about sex amongst adults was about, and began to wonder if we had even done things correctly.

Needless to say, I'd been in no hurry to repeat such a performance, and had ended my relationship with Daniel soon afterwards.

***

I must have eventually fallen asleep because I am either dead or dreaming when the sound of a horse's thundering hooves pierce my unconscious mind.

I sit up in bed as the sound quietens, then picks up volume again. Starlight has been gone for years, and the hooves beating powerful circles into the meadow are not his dainty gallop. I can hear some excited giggles from outside my bedroom door and in a wave of confusion, I pull the blankets off and run to the window. As I pull back the heavy drapes I see Michael, standing in the meadow, while a black and white horse canters in circles around him. Michael holds the lunge rein taut and clicks, to which the horse responds in an obedient, muscular canter.

Once again, I hear Izzy's uncontained giggles and the squeak of floorboards as she hovers outside my door.

'EYEBROWS!' I yell at her, and she is in like a flash, my freshly brushed wig in one hand and makeup bag in the other.

It takes me a long time to get ready and my annoyance at seeing Michael sitting in the kitchen talking to Mother abates the instant he looks up at me. No wheelchair.

'Anna.' He stands up and with only a slight limp, walks towards me as she scuttles into the conservatory. His hair is blond and shaved very close to his head, like a new army recruit. His eyes are bright and bluey grey, perhaps a little worried-looking.

'You look so beautiful,' he says, and I *feel* beautiful under his ardent stare. I step forward and he reaches out to hold my hand. For a moment I think he is going to shake it, but he pulls me towards him and I swear a thousand fireworks go off somewhere in the world as we fall into our first real kiss.

His mouth sets my whole body on fire until he pulls back and plants hard kisses on my jaw and my neck. 'God, woman.' He breathes and my legs feel unsteady. 'I've missed you.'

We pry apart and I look up at him, smiling. 'I can't believe you're here. I was so unkind to you.'

'I accept the exceptional circumstances. You've got a brain tumour; you didn't know what you were saying.'

I laugh because we both know I knew exactly what I was saying.

'Anyway, I always wanted a stroppy, seriously ill, crazy girlfriend and you trump all those departments!'

I don't hear ill or crazy or stroppy ... I just hear 'girlfriend'.

'Well, I always wanted an annoying boyfriend with spinal damage. Who listens to *everything* my mother tells him!'

And that was that, we were Michael and Anna. Together despite everything, and apparently thanks to Mother, because she had called him yesterday and said I might like to see him. Perhaps she has *slightly* redeemed herself.

I am pleased to see a fair-sized bag under the breakfast bar. It seems like he plans to stay a few nights, although he must have feared I would send him packing.

I suddenly remember the horse. 'Michael, did you ride here?'

'No!' he says, laughing. 'I came in the horsebox with a surprise for you.' We wander out the back door, through the little rose garden and into the meadow. 'This is Pinto; he's a beauty, no? You can try western riding, like you said you wanted to.'

I look up at the sixteen-hand horse and think that sounded like a much better idea when I was snuggling up to Michael in the day room, trying to sound adventurous. 'Ooh I'd love to ride in a real western saddle. I haven't ridden since I was fourteen, but Father said I was a natural.'

I remember silently, 'A natural at flying through the air.'

'Don't be afraid, Anna.'

He must have seen my expression so I try to look less worried and tell him, 'Maybe tomorrow, I have a sore head today. Will he be OK in the meadow?'

Michael doesn't look like he believes me but he must not want to burst our happy bubble so he just smiles and says, 'Sure. He lives out at home. I'll just check his water and we can leave saddling him up until the morning; when you feel better.'

I am quite certain that I will still have a headache, and that it will possibly be slightly worse tomorrow.

***

My Father greets Michael with a death-grip handshake and a rather menacing stare. 'Well, nice to meet you, Michael. Unfortunately, I'm off to Leeds on business for a few days, so err ... watch yourselves now.'

Izzy is pulling faces behind his back and Michael and I try hard to stifle our laughter. My father has a very stiff upper lip, and very few social skills. Still, he takes my apparent joy and this new arrival as his excuse to take leave from the tense household for a while, hoping he will not be too missed.

My mother breezes past and smiles pleasantly at us. 'Izzy and I are dropping your father off at the station, and then we're going to dinner and a show. We'll be back late.' She half smiles and I can barely believe she is behaving almost human and giving Michael and I some time alone; although she could have been a bit more subtle about it.

As soon as they leave, an excruciatingly painful shyness descends upon me. The grandfather clock in the hall ticks in loud echoes, as though enhancing my nervous silence.

'Are you hungry?' I ask him.

'No. Are you?' He's half smiling again.

'No. I can't remember what hungry feels like.'

'I can.' He stares at me and I give an involuntary shake of pleasure. Or nerves. I'm not sure which.

'Would you like me to show you the house?' I

had heard Father saying this haughtily to his guests and copied his impressive tone.

'Show me your bedroom.' It is almost a whisper and I feel like my legs might fail me as I lead up the long sweeping staircases. Thankfully, the heavy curtains are still mostly closed and I feel relieved that it casts a more flattering light on both the dishevelled room and my pain-ravaged body.

He pulls me towards him once more and there is nothing else to do but accept my fear and live through it. Fear that he will see my thin body and be repulsed, fear I cannot make the wild love he may be expecting or that it might hurt as it had before. Daniel had left me disappointed and used, like someone had taken a beautiful silk scarf and blown their nose on it. I close my eyes and my thoughts mercifully lift, little dandelion wisps being carried away on a breeze, as he kisses me until all of my doubts drift away.

I lift my arms as he pulls my dress slowly over my hips and my head. I grasp at his T-shirt and breathe gently over his lean, strong body. I run my palms down the firm muscles of his chest and arms.

We move towards the bed and he lies me down gently. It feels right that he is taking control, pausing for a moment to look at my naked body as I lie shyly beneath him. While he watches me with hazy eyes, I silently pray he will not ask me to take off my wig. He doesn't. Instead, he kisses from my neck to my navel, hard kisses that speak louder than words we no longer require.

I am absorbed in every moment of his exploring lips but I have a greater need, and pull him towards me to kiss him with urgency.

When Michael is inside me, I forget everything else.

I almost laugh with sheer joy as this new feeling consumes my entire being. It is beautiful, and as cliché as it sounds, I know this is the difference. It's beautiful because I love him.

I'll take my chance to be happy. Whether it's for the next few hours or days, I do not care, because when we are together like this, I have become someone else. I am his and he is mine, and we have found something that matters. For the first time in my life I feel a sense of contentment and heart-aching happiness, and it feels so right maybe I do deserve it.

***

A little while later he looks down at me and brushes the falling hair from my face with his fingers. I try to discreetly scratch my scalp.

'Is it bothering you?'

'A little, now I've been hot under it!' I feel comfortable enough to let him ease the wig from my head and take off the netting underneath.

'Beautiful.' He smiles so honestly that I almost believe him. My hair is barely there, but it's growing back just a little. I'm not entirely bald.

'Shall we go riding? It's a perfect time. Sunset.'

I hesitate for a second, not wanting to disappoint my new-found love. He does not give me time to think of an excuse, as he leaves the room quickly, telling me to wrap up warm.

I touch up my makeup, try to find some warm clothes that are both sexy *and* sensible, and run to find him in the meadow with Pinto.

Pinto really is a beauty. He is black and white with a long, silky black mane that reaches far down past his neck. He looks like one of the painted horses Native Americans would ride into battle.

I reach up tentatively and stroke his neck. 'Should we be riding when we're ill?'

Michael just smiles and adjusts the reins, leading the horse to the fence. 'I can't ride yet. You'll have to do it for me. Don't worry, I'll lunge him so you'll just go in steady circles.'

I still feel very dubious as he holds my hand and I climb onto the second rung of the fence.

'Put your foot here.' He holds out the Western-style stirrup and I place my one hand on the pommel and the other on the back of the huge saddle. I swing my leg over and settle down gently; remembering how Starlight hated it when we landed heavily in her saddle. I find my balance and Michael places my other foot in the stirrup. I look up through Pinto's forward-pointing ears and see the sun beginning her low descent into the silver birch forest ahead. I look at Michael and as his eyes meet mine, I realise I have the biggest smile on my face I can remember.

We start in slow circles, and my fear dissipates as I feel the cocooning comfort of the saddle. As Pinto's pace changes from walk to slow trot, I laugh as I forget to rise and stay low in the saddle.

'I love it much more than English riding!'

'Of course.' Michael tries to sound cool, but I can tell he's delighted. 'Think you can go solo?'

My nerves flutter, but only for a second before I nod bravely. I can do this by myself.

As Michael unclips the lunge rein, I guide Pinto away from him and we walk gently to the far edge of the meadow. As we turn back around, I see the sunset breaking into magnificent oranges and gold, and my heart lifts once more. If someone had told me a few months ago I would be riding a beautiful horse into the sunset with no hair under my cowboy hat, I would have thought they were insane. I could never change places with the old me now, and I tap my heels with urgency so Pinto picks up my command and breaks into an easy canter towards the setting sun.

If you have never cantered a horse, you need to. It is the most exhilarating feeling as you hear the steady, pounding hooves and sway with the rocking motion of the magnificent gait.

If the end of something, like the end of this day, could be so beautiful, perhaps I had nothing to fear after all.

*   *   *

As night falls and Pinto has been groomed, blanketed, and fed, we leave him nibbling the grass and swishing his tail. Walking hand-in-hand to the kitchen, I tell Michael he is no longer my true love.

'Let me guess, you love the horse more, right?'

'Yep.' I laugh and hit him with the cowboy hat he brought me, seemingly oblivious to the fact that I look less than respectable with no hair.

'I knew you'd like him, he's one of my favourites too.'

He tells me about the horses, including a palomino like the one in the picture he had given me in hospital...

'I tore it up.' I blurt out my guilty secret

'You were hurt; I can get you another one.'

'I'd really like that. You don't know how happy it made me when you gave me the picture. I felt it was all so doomed, out of my control.'

'Well,' he changes the subject, 'they are one of the most beautiful horses in the world. We have a Palomino on the ranch; I'm the only one who rides her.'

'Why only you?'

'She is quite flighty, always on her toes but I seem to have a calming influence.' He looks at me sideways and I hope he is not comparing me to a highly strung horse.

'I'd like to see her one day.'

Michael smiles and ends the conversation, to my pleasure, with a kiss.

***

By the time Izzy and Mother got back, we were drinking hot chocolate in front of the fire. I was so content I even poured Lillian a glass of wine and she happily joined us. The moment was instantly ruined when she let out an exasperated cry as Michael told her I had been riding.

'Really, Michael, I'm surprised. I thought you brought the animal to *show* her, not for her to go galloping around the fields. Some days she can barely walk.'

My eyebrows knitted together crossly as he tried to explain, 'Pinto is my gentlest horse, Mrs. Winters. A child could ride him.'

Once again she had ruined everything. My sense of accomplishment at cantering into the sunset for the first time on a new horse with a strange saddle, deflated like an old balloon. A child could have done it.

No one noticed me get up to leave as Michael tried to defend his actions and insisted I was safe. Mother humiliated me further by telling him I am not a competent rider and what would have happened if I had fallen off? They both sounded very upset and I could have screamed Elm Tree to the ground that my beautiful memory had been ruined, and I was to be discussed like this – an invalid once more.

Izzy finds me in the kitchen sneaking a glass of Mother's wine. I have taken two more tablets but they do nothing.

'Have you taken your proper medication? Not the painkillers, the other ones?'

'Every morning,' I mutter. Mr Raj had given me a stern discussion regarding my home medication; I was too frightened not to take everything exactly as he had prescribed. It was only the sedative painkillers I used against his instruction.

'She just worries about you, Anna.' Izzy knows Mother has blown it once more. 'She's told Michael if he saddles Pinto again he must leave this house.'

I glare at Izzy, guessing she agrees with our mother. 'Tell Michael I need to lie down for a little while.'

Izzy kisses my cheek and I am too exhausted to worry about leaving her alone with him. I use the last of my strength to make it upstairs and crawl under my blankets.

I know my father will be expecting Michael to sleep in one of our guest rooms, but while sleep evades me I'm happy to hear him come into my room and slip into bed beside me. We make love and his strength soothes my troubled soul. I kiss his mouth and ask him if he loves me.

'Yes, Anna. I love you.' I smile contentedly and fall soundly asleep.

The following day, Michael left to go to the hospital for physiotherapy and have the last of his stitches removed. That left me with an anxious-looking mother, as I had barely spoken to her since she forbade my riding.

'We have two more days until the operation, is there anything you would like to do?'

'Any last requests?' I couldn't resist the nasty joke.

'I was going to take you to Northampton but your grandfather is still too poorly, and now Grandma is unwell also. Cheryl and Natasha sent you a lovely card this morning, but they're in Newcastle with their mother. Isabel is out today so perhaps we could do something just the two of us? I know Michael will be back tomorrow so I won't see much of you then.'

She finally paused to take a breath and eye me with caution.

'I'm meeting Jules and Eddie,' I said firmly, although I had only decided to in that instant. The thought of spending possibly my second last day alive with my depressed, overbearing mother was not an option.

I left her alone in the hallway and ran upstairs to find my phone. A little whistle signalled a new message and I smiled as Michael reminded me to feed Pinto. I texted him that of course I will, and then add that I miss him, before scrolling down to Jules' number.

'We're in the Whistling Duck!' She already sounded drunk, and I tell her I would be there in an hour.

Mother appeared in my doorway. 'Anna, do you really think it's a good idea to meet up with those two today? You know they'll be drinking and you have to be so careful on your medication. Can you not take it easy and wait for Michael?'

I snorted and was already pulling a dress over my head, trying not to mess up my wig.

'At least let me take you. I'll drive you and pick you up later.'

'Stop it, Mother! Please stop treating me like an invalid. I can meet them. I can catch a bus to see my friends and make my own way home! I'm not dead yet. Just because you're happy cooped up in this mausoleum all day does not mean I want to stay here with you. Now more than ever!'

For the second time that day I leave her looking bereft as I grab my bag and push past her. I hope she does not see me as I have to steady myself on the landing and a new wave of dizziness overcomes me.

I take a few deep breaths and head out of the door to walk unsteadily down Elm Tree Lane. I do not feel at all well, and I hear Mr Raj's stern voice telling me I needed to spend my time in a complete state of rest.

My legs are trembling as I turn back towards my childhood home. I see my mother standing at the landing window watching me, and I try to call out to her, but my final thought as I crash to the floor is that I have forgotten to feed Pinto.

PART TWO

'In the night of death, hope sees a star
And listening love can hear the rustle of a
wing.'

Robert G Ingersoll

CHAPTER SIX:

LIFE AFTER LIFE

A pulse echoes through my body. Not my heart or the pain that has been so grimly persistent at my temples, it is a pounding beat getting louder and louder. A separate force is pulling the base of my neck, forcing me into an upright position. All sense of normality and reality abandon me as I am lifted up and turned over to see myself lying on the hospital bed. That is definitely me. Wretched and pale, and although I am still wearing my green dress, *she* is lying naked, covered to the chest with a pale blue sheet. I hear a droning beep from a machine to the right, and a strange clamp is fitted to my skull, standing by which, both dressed in surgical gowns, are Mr Raj and another man I've never seen before.

I am standing at the base of the bed and I struggle to hear, as they are talking with muffled voices covered by masks. The buzzing increases and vibrations begin to fill the air. A nurse is heading towards me and I stand strong, I already know she will not see me. Only her eyes are visible as she too wears a white mask and her hair is covered, but they are beautiful and dark, with long, thick lashes. Her brows are perfectly arched like a screen siren from the fifties. As envisaged, she walks straight through me, and I try to tune out the intense buzzing but it is impossible. I close my eyes as the vibrations become ever more pervasive, and I hear her say before a great rush carries me away, 'Those flowers remind me there is beauty in this world.'

***

I'm surrounded by light, inescapably cocooned in a ball of comfort and illumination. I feel something that is impossible to express, as I accept that my life is over yet my journey has not been ended. I begin to feel incredible peace, and the light that enfolds me speaks in a language of acceptance and love. I think I wish to remain here for all eternity, but my body is moving on and I think of dandelions being carried away on the breeze. I am a Chinese lantern floating softly among a never ending sky of brilliant diamonds. The movement is constant, with a purpose, and from the depth of my being I am conscious of still existing while I move further and further away from Michael, my family, and all I've known to be life.

I feel not a moment of sadness.

As I drift with no expectation through the unending light, I see a Being that seems to be made up of sparkling crystals. It moves in perfect sync with me, an almost human shape, with the same head and four limbs, but much taller and leaner and made up of only illuminations. I am mesmerised.

The Being communicates telepathically and I find my new language in response to him; not words exactly, but sounds and vibrations thought to one another. I sense a gentle maleness about him and he tells me that he is my Guide.

This was happening to me. I was neither dreaming nor hallucinating, and far from being dead, I had never felt more alive.

***

The Guide continues in this same rippling movement, in one direction and with determined focus. Communication has ceased and my thoughts and feelings seem separate from my being. I cannot rationalise, panic nor feel elated. I am being taken along like a fallen leaf on a fast flowing river. I think I was becoming quite accustomed to this charming experience when it ended very suddenly and I find myself standing alone, sense and emotion returned. I feel I have been awakened and now possess knowledge of unknown depths. My journey through light has told me that I have come home, to a place where illness can no longer torture my soul.

The most beautiful view of a valley is before me, with rolling meadows and fields upon fields of long grass showcasing wild flowers that dance in the gentle breeze. I've been here before. I'm certain. This feels like somewhere on earth. Can you remember a time when you have visited somewhere heart achingly beautiful? Like a white beach on a Mediterranean island, where you can walk a hundred yards out into the turquoise ocean and the water is still crystal clear? Or woodlands with thick carpets of pine needles where sunlight twinkles through the heavy canopies above? Did you think those places felt like heaven? That they are so calming and serene that you feel inspired to believe this cruel life may be worth living after all?

I look out and breathe in the true beauty of the universe, and walk through the long grass towards the sounds of a stream running over stones in dips and troughs. I feel young, and I quicken my pace; clusters of wild poppies remind me of Elm Tree.

A small boy is leaning over the water. He turns and waves as he hears me approaching, and it feels perfectly natural that I should go straight to him.

'I'm Anna,' I say with more than a little uncertainty as I find I am using words again rather than thoughts.

He looks only six or seven, and says nothing, just leans further over the water.

'What are you doing?'

'I'm waiting for Michael.' He looks at me and I see it in his face. I know him instantly.

'You're Benji?'

'Please don't call me that. I'm not a Collie. Ben is fine, or Benjamin. Ben is better.'

'Michael told me about you, that you drowned and he couldn't save you.'

'I know. I'm waiting for him and when he comes I will tell him he never needed to feel all that guilt, I chose to stay here. I didn't want to go back.'

***

I wanted to ask Ben more, but he had started to frown so I didn't press him. 'Do you stay here by yourself and wait for him?'

He looks at me like I'm crazy. 'Of course not. I have very important things to do. I just come here when I need to think, and The Sphere can be a hard place to concentrate.'

'It's not that different from your reality. People wait for each other, and when they come they need somewhere to go, right? You could stay here for ever if you want to, or you can go back.' He juts out his chin determinedly, reminding me of Michael. 'I'm not going back,' he says proudly. 'I'm going to be a Guide. I've advanced far enough now, my last task is to free my brother of his pain then I'll move on to the next level.'

'How many levels are there?' I want this young boy to tell me everything he knows.

'Only three to concern yourself with.' He draws three lines in the ground beneath us. 'This is the middle level, most people come here. These are people who are essentially good. They might have lied, cheated, stolen, or even robbed a bank. But the human frailties that lead to such mistakes are forgiven. If you don't learn from your mistakes and seek forgiveness during your earth life, then you must learn from them here. Once you have become learned, and completed your tasks, you can go back to being human, stay here, or advance to the highest levels. You can guide lost souls from there or watch over loved ones. You can communicate with the awakened on earth and you can teach. I want to Guide.'

This enlightenment is strangely familiar. 'Is the lower level like Hell?'

'It is not the Hell you've been taught to imagine, but you wouldn't want to be there for very long. Very bad people go there, all the dark souls. They have to face the things they've done wrong and experience the pain they inflicted on others. When they are truly sorry, and forgiven by those they have wronged, they may begin to advance towards the light. As superior beings we seek progression – no soul was born to stay still. Even the most microscopic entities strive to grow and advance; it is the way of the universe.'

I must look uncertain as he goes on to tell me, 'Beings are forgiven, Anna, because that is natural progression. Bad people are bad for reasons we may never understand, but they have free will the same as all of us and if they choose to seek forgiveness and advancement then they shall. If not, they simply stay in the darkness. All the things people do on earth are a mere prelude to a journey that begins here. Life on earth is about learning. Learning to love rather than hate and to help one another with acts of kindness and compassion. After you've spent some time here, you'll wonder why so many find such simplicity so difficult. Why everything's so messed up.'

'Maybe because life is painful and cruel, Ben.' I am starting to feel a little cross with this child, talking like a wizened man of a hundred. It is unnerving when someone so much younger has overtaken your knowledge. For some reason, I am reminded of my grandma frantically pressing every button on the remote control in search of the right one. She would always get teletext instead of *EastEnders*, or the TV guide instead of *Countdown*. Then she would look at me as I swiped it impatiently from her and put it right. Grandma always hated the advancement of technology, saying that things were best left alone.

Ben was making me empathise with her; he was calm and knowing and I was overwhelmed as he continued. 'Life isn't easy. People have bad parents, bad relationships. People get sick. Without realising it, they become bitter and their fear and resentment feed the anger so they do bad things. Other people have the strength to move on from a sad place, and follow the truth inside their hearts. I know some who had terrible childhoods that went on to live happy, fulfilled lives, becoming wonderful parents themselves. They are enlightened and progression comes to some more naturally than others, but all the same it is available to each and every one of us.'

'Do you really think life can be simple? Can people find happiness through their pain?'

'You did, Anna. You got sick, then you found love. Maybe you have more to learn.' He looks behind him, then back to me. 'It would seem as though you do.'

'What you said about standing still, I often felt like that before I was ill, like every day was the same ... starting with an alarm piercing my dreams and ending with a collapse into bed. Where was my progression? I was just a hamster on a wheel doing the same thing over and over.'

Ben smiles and tells me so many people were the doing exactly that. 'But think about it.' He turns to look at me with beautiful dark eyes. 'You were a baby needing constant care, then you grew stronger and more independent as your body changed in to a child and then into a young woman. Progression begins from the moment you are conceived, and it is affected by the influences around you as you grow. These are different for all of us. Good families, bad families, rich, poor. Those influences are endless, but there is only one thing that can truly navigate how much or little you progress.'

I nod as I understand. It is down to each one of us, how hard we struggle and fight for the life we desire, or how much easier we may find it to simply drift and hope things will turn out OK. It had been down to me to progress to my full potential and I had chosen not to.

Even when my life was to be taken away from me, deep down I knew I was still drifting. I could have fought against the tide but it seemed too strong for me. I even let Michael go when he talked of hope with my mother and told me I might survive. I had *chosen* not to fight.

Michael didn't give up on me; he came back to Elm Tree with Pinto. He was brave. Perhaps that is why he is still living and I find myself here with Ben.

Ben reads my mind and says gently, 'You could have been more positive during your illness, Anna, but you couldn't have cured it. You were meant to come here – it is the life you lived before that which you need to analyse now. It would be better if you thought about changing your perspective while you are here.' He turns to face me, sitting crossed-legged on the sandy shore.

'Imagine if at the point of death, everyone had a chance to look over their lives and consider what they would have done differently. If every person who consistently did bad things suddenly stopped and learned to live through the light, do you think they would be given a second chance to keep on living?

'Can you imagine a drunk father beating his child, suddenly dropping to his knees with true remorse and promising to only give love and comfort from that day on? Or if every world leader took care of their people and made sure they could live in a land without poverty, famine, or war? Imagine there was no need to feel superior, from a mouse to a lion to a neighbour of lesser means. We are all children of the same stars, Anna.'

'Children of the same stars?' I contemplate his words and feel the power of the immense universe around me. How comforting to think that all life forms I had ever seen or known were part of a kin. An overwhelming prospect even for someone who had died, yet I talked and breathed still. I saw a tiny green bug scuttling in the grass next to my bare feet, and felt a rush of a guilt that I may have flicked him away before I realised he had as much right to live as I did; That he began his little life as I had, tiny and vulnerable, following the progression of nature to thrive and grow. Wherever we began, we certainly end up at the same eventuality.

Ben watches my eyes following the creature and smiles. 'Everything has its place. All things are connected.'

'So what else?' I ask him, finding such happiness in his simple words, depicting the answers to questions we already know deep within ourselves.

'The universe gives birth to life you cannot even begin to imagine, but think of the trees, animals, and people you have walked passed in your lifetime without consideration that they are your kin, part of an intricate network within which we are one family. Each with our place that makes us connect and most importantly, progress. To understand, to live and breathe such truth is the path to enlightenment.'

I look at Benji, wondering how someone so young can speak with such certainty.

'Isn't that just idealistic? People will always be cruel. It's in our nature to think only of ourselves, no one really cares about other people. Leaders cause famine and war, spouses cheat, and people kill. I've seen children throw rocks at birds and stamp on wild flowers. The world can be so terrible, Ben, you would never know where to start! Where would you even begin to make it better?' I close my eyes as vibrations begin to stir and escalate all around me.

He stands up and I keep my eyes closed as his

strong little voice is carried away on the heightened buzzing. 'With you, Anna. All they want is for it to begin with you.'

***

When I open my eyes Benji has gone and I feel lost. Where was my sense of peace? That boundless joy I had felt only moments ago. It was slipping away and I was ever more conscious of a pulling deep inside my stomach.

I began to realise that I *had* lost the life I knew. I wouldn't see Michael for a very long time; he would be waiting now outside the operating theatre with my parents, in one of those awful rooms reserved for relatives. A doctor would open the door and they would all look up expectantly, eyes red with tears of fear; fears that would soon be justified.

'We did everything we could for Anna, but I'm sorry, she didn't survive the procedure.'

I imagine my mother putting her hand to her mouth, making a strangled sound.

I hear the noise of something large moving through the long grass behind us. I don't feel fear, exactly, but I am certainly unnerved as I see two magnificent beasts, similar to wolves but much larger, and made up again of those dazzling lights. I spin around so my eyes can follow their movements as they continue to the shore of the lake, less than fifteen feet between us.

I sense vibrations channelling between them, and know it is their communication I am feeling. I have lost my voice, acknowledging there is no choice but to remain silent.

One wolf is dark, a shimmering blackened grey. I do not have a bad feeling from him, but when his shining eyes focus on me I look quickly and respectfully away. I know I am inferior to this being, that he is much more powerful than me in every sense.

He turns his head away and they drink from the cool waters till their actions create ripples in the water. I am totally transfixed and as I stare into the lake, its surface becomes glass-like and I am shocked to make out the scene of a classroom. As the ripples begin to settle, I see that it is my old classroom and three rows from the back, there I am. Anna Winters, aged fourteen and a half.

At first I am fascinated by the images until a slow, sweeping feeling of dread overcomes me as I recognise the day that the scene is playing out. This was a time in my life I had desperately, desperately tried to forget and I fought to tear my eyes away, to beg the wolves to make it stop, but I was alone. There was darkness surrounding me and I was not being permitted to take my eyes from the images, forced to relive each moment.

***

I was very popular at school before sixth form, before I outgrew most of my peers. My parents were incredibly wealthy and I always had the most fashionable clothes and the latest accessories to go with them. Amongst our elite and competitive group of peers, we were far more into our looks and our possessions than our class work and studies. High school for us was simply our stage, our catwalk, and our own soap opera.

I suppose there were about twelve of us who had clicked since middle school. Tina Westwood was my best friend, and of the twelve there were five boys who we deemed fit to interchangeably date and break up with. Daniel was my preferred choice and I revolved most of my time around flirting with him then being very cross at him moments later. At that time, nothing ever went beyond the occasional kiss, but it was all great fun and we thought we were the epitome of cool walking down the corridors hand in hand.

As the more popular girls in school are, there were times when we could be more than a little cruel, especially when we were all together. We just felt invincible. I had a particularly mean streak and don't know where it came from, but I carried around a lot of aggression. I wish I had some excusable reason for my behaviour, like I had been beaten by my parents or bullied as a younger child, but there is nothing I can remember. At times I was just inexcusably nasty.

Maria Stapleton was not a popular girl. She was almost completely blind, and when she spoke to you her slightly cloudy eyes focused somewhere beyond where you were standing. Maria had a school assistant who went everywhere with her, and this was where a lot of the problems started. Her assistant was *huge*. She clambered behind Maria, bumping into our tables and chairs with her colossal hips. I suppose she was quite young and sweet, probably mid-twenties with a quiet disposition that contradicted her size. In a dreary lesson, with a bored-looking teacher droning on about algebra, Maria and her helper were our favoured source of entertainment. I used to pretend to struggle with a sum and ask the assistant for help while one of our crew swapped her chair for a broken one. She would sit back down and go crashing to the floor, skirt billowing around her ample thighs and Maria would get the fright of her life at the clattering noise. We would convulse in hysterics while the hurt-looking woman would try to compose herself.

I use to stick Post-its on the back of Maria's school jumper and wrote words I shouldn't repeat. Daniel and I liked to sneak up behind her when she was sitting alone outside at lunchtimes and suddenly shout things in her ear. She would give out a little scream and we'd shove her roughly and say we were only messing. I once spent a lesson flicking bits of screwed up paper at her and as the boys around me laughed, the paper was flicked harder till she was literally jumping out of her seat.

Her parents knew she was being bullied because one day, Maria did not attend school and our registration period was interrupted by the Headmaster. Mr Langley could strike a pang of fear in even the boldest of teenage hearts, and we all fell silent as he ranted at the front of the classroom about our intolerable behaviour. He mentioned unacceptable conduct and told us if he had received specific names then the offenders would be punished.

'Some of you seem to think you have means of authority within this classroom that supersedes our school policy and code of conduct.' To my absolute horror, he was making an obvious point of staring directly at me. I tried my utter hardest to look nonchalant but I felt my cheeks starting to burn and everyone watch me intently. This obviously had the desired effect, because his burning eyes never left me and he was shouting with increased anger. 'Some of you seem to think it is OK to make someone else feel too afraid to come to my school! What gives you the right to make a person feel that way? Are they different to your perfect self? If I receive the names of these culprits, which I have every intention of doing, I will be forced to punish them. This will result in permanent exclusion, and a blackened mark for ever against their name as a bully.' A gasp emanates from my captivated audience but his tirade is losing a little of its venom. He shrugs his shoulders as my eyes fill with tears and my peers stare harder.

'Some of you seem to think you are better than others. But the truth is, and one day everyone will see this, the truth is that some of you are rotten to the core.'

I was literally burning with humiliation. Not shame at this point, just hate for singling me out so obviously, and I hated Maria Stapleton more than you could possibly imagine. She had humiliated me in front of everyone, and I knew they would never forget this.

Of course Maria knew our names and I wondered why she didn't give them. Maybe she knew it would only make things worse. Things got worse anyway, horribly worse.

For two days it transpired that she would not be coming to school with her assistant. She would be as independent as she was at home, and relying on her cane to guide her around the building, with the teachers offering extra support until a new helper was allocated. One can hardly blame the last one for throwing in the towel; I was surprised she hadn't left sooner.

This made Maria an easy target, not that anyone dared to say anything to her now. She just sat two rows in front of me, looking like every fibre in her body was tensed, anticipating the inevitable attack.

I was still seething but I knew I had to tone it down; I couldn't go through another face off with the Head like that.

I just wanted the last word, a final laugh at her expense or something to hurt her, like she had hurt me.

The teacher was writing on the whiteboard, her back to us. Everyone else was copying her words, looking down at their books as they scribbled away. This was my chance. I dropped my pen so it rolled down the classroom towards her table. I crept forward and as I knelt down beside her in the pretence of picking it up, I whispered nastily in her ear, 'It's such a good thing you're blind so you can't see how ugly you really are.'

With a smirk on my face and a few pupils raising their eyebrows at me, I returned to my seat and hummed a little satisfied tune under my breath as I finish the paragraph I was writing. I look up a few moments later to see Maria staring straight ahead and completely motionless, apart from a single tear falling from her pale eyes and making a slow trail down her slender cheek. In that instant I was hit by a crashing tornado of shame, and it has never, ever left me.

The tear from her cheek falls onto the ground that is now the lake. My tears are flowing freely and the water where I am kneeling collects them and carries each one away on the ebbing tide. I have felt her pain, a pain so acute I am overcome once more with guilt I could ever have caused it.

The images disperse and I am relieved to be away from the school and those terrible memories, but I feel so alone in this strange place that appears to be my life after death. The darkness is receding and within moments I feel the presence of a young woman beside me, and without turning to look at her I know it is Maria.

***

During my second year of sixth form I received an email from Tina asking me if I remembered Maria and did I know she had been killed by a drunk driver. I recall staring at the computer screen and being unable to move for a long time.

The feelings of guilt and regret had come flooding back, surpassing them the now irreversible fact that I had never found a way to apologise to Maria during what was left of our school years. She never acknowledged me again after the day I whispered in her ear. She made me feel invisible during a time when she blossomed and even made a few friends. In Year Eleven she started to wear a cool pair of Ray-Bans and would throw her long, chestnut hair over her shoulders, laughing while the boys in our class made exaggerated protests that they should be able to wear shades in class too. She grew tall and slender, and started to wear glossy pink lipstick which was breaking the school rules. One day I asked her if I could borrow some as she applied it expertly to her mouth, but she turned her head and started chatting to Daniel. I remember Tina looking impressed. She had never seen someone dare to snub me, and I scowled gloomily for the rest of the day.

The last time I saw Maria Stapleton she was in the park one summer, with a beautiful golden Labrador in a guide dog harness talking to a young man I supposed was her boyfriend. She must have been almost seventeen and looked so happy, laughing in a carefree manner. I started to walk towards them, thinking maybe now she would listen to me, I wanted to say sorry and unburden myself of this ugly guilt. I wanted to tell her I had never treated anyone like that since I saw her crying, and she would see I had changed.

As I got nearer though, I lost my courage. She had this way of making me feel small and invisible. I paused for a long time but eventually I turned around and walked away from them.

***

'Hello, Anna.' She is beside me, and for the first time since I have sensed her presence I turn to look at her, noticing that the dark wolf has gone and only the bright one is lying watching us, a little closer to the shore.

'Maria, I never thought I'd see you again.'

'We can see whoever we choose to here.'

'You chose to see me?'

For the first time, she lifts her head up and looks at me through beautiful aquamarine eyes. She holds my gaze and I take in her beauty. I suppose she was always beautiful but I never saw past her blindness. This loveliness was not limited to her appearance and her now exquisite eyes, it radiated from her, from somewhere deep within her soul. I felt a very human pang of envy and sorrow, as I realized I would never possess this nature of beauty. I look down at my hands as I imagine how I must look beside her.

'When I heard you were here, Anna, I wanted to see you. I wanted to tell you I'm sorry.'

I am completely taken aback. 'Why would you need to apologise to me? I behaved terribly; I never forgave myself for the things I said to you, the things I did. I called you ugly; I threw things and shouted at you ...' My voice trails away as I suddenly consider she might be making fun of me somehow, she looks so peaceful and self-assured.

'Yes. You did hurt me, you really did. I used to cry every night after school. I'd pray to make things better, to make me invisible to you.'

I hang my head in shame as she continues. 'Actually, my mother came in one night before I went to bed and begged me to tell her what was happening. She knew I could barely eat or sleep and she told me she could hear me crying in my room at night. I confided in her about some of what was happening, but I was too afraid to mention names, I knew that would lead to more trouble.' She met my eyes again. 'You hated me so much already. I think my mother went into school and they said they'd look out for any signs of bullying. It was the teachers who realized it was you, Anna. I didn't tell them.'

I look out to the lake as she continued, 'After the day you whispered in my ear, I decided if God wouldn't make me invisible to you, then I would make *you* invisible to me. I didn't know where your hate towards me came from and I no longer cared. It was your problem, not mine. In fact, it made me stronger. I decided I no longer needed an assistant; I wanted to be independent. My support group had told me they had a dog for me who would guide me after I'd completed my GCSEs and they took me to see him as a puppy. He lived with us after his training. I fell in love with him at once and he guided me for nearly three years before I died – My very best friend.'

I listen to her voice fill with warmth and love as she talks about her dog. It had surprised me that it had been her decision not to have assistance at school. I was surprised and impressed by her bravery.

'He wasn't with me the night I died. I had been out for dinner with friends and thought I could manage alone. I'm glad he wasn't there, he couldn't have saved me. The car came from nowhere and crashed onto the kerb when I was about to cross. He would have been killed also.' A tear falls from her lovely eyes and she smiles sadly. 'I still feel lost without his senses to guide me. I would have liked him here with me, Anna, but it wasn't his time. I think he was needed to help someone else.' She frowns and I ask her what is wrong.

'We used to connect with each other often, he pined for me and I was able to comfort him. Animals are much more aware than we could ever be. As we grow older we are manipulated so much by the world around us, we are *taught* what to believe that we forget to use the insight we were born with. I can often reach animals and very young children, but rarely grown-ups.' She shakes her head and the little frown deepens. 'I haven't been able to reach him, he is getting old and I fear he is in jeopardy.' She touches the water in front of us, which ripples then returns to cool stillness.

'Nothing.'

We sit quietly for a little while as I don't know how to comfort her. I wish I could. I break the silence eventually, 'What did you call your friend?'

'Marley,' she says, a smile breaking through her saddened features at the sound of his name.

'So we really do all come here. Even animals?' I wonder where my beloved Tulip might be.

Maria is clearly another one to communicate in telepathy for she laughs gently and tells me, 'Your little friend is here somewhere, Anna. But it is only those that we truly connected with, on an eternal and spiritual level, we are reunited with in the immediate afterlife. You can wait for your loved ones to come, or find them waiting for you, and all the while you learn to live with the intuition you were born with before life begins to take it all away. I'm learning forgiveness, and that's why I came to find you. To tell you that I'm sorry I didn't forgive you when I knew you were sorry for what you had done.'

'How did you know? I was never brave enough to tell you.'

'When you lose one sense, your others become heightened. The energy when you were near me changed, your voice was different, the way you behaved. I knew you were sorry. I just wanted to punish you.'

'I was sorry, Maria. I'm still sorry.'

'Don't be,' she says, placing my hand on top of hers. 'We were young, and if I hadn't been so stubborn we might have even been friends. Perhaps we're friends now, after all.'

I reach towards her and she puts her slender arms around me. We hold onto each other tightly as I cry helplessly on her shoulder, my body wracked with relief as her energy dissolves all the shame. As she strokes my back I hiccup loudly and my tears turn to sudden giggles till we're both laughing uncontrollably. I open my swollen eyes over her shoulder to see the bright wolf look briefly towards me, bowing its beautiful head before walking away.

***

I must have fallen asleep because I wake up alone. I open my eyes to a sky of magnificent blue. It reminded me of those glorious summer days when everything almost seems to stand still. There are only endless sapphire skies, and the occasional sound of laughter is carried towards you by a gentle wind. I step towards the lake and cup my hands to drink from the cool waters. As I lean forward I catch my refection looking back at me. I have long, dark blonde hair, my natural colour, and my skin is bright and glowing. I have thick eyelashes which frame my eyes, all the greyish traces of illness gone. I'm wearing my green dress and see that I was lovely once more. I feel at peace again within my new existence. I know that Maria is gone, but the memory of our talk and laughter filled me with contentment.

I decide to stop waiting by the lake and want to try and find Ben. I still have a lot of questions for him. As I follow a footpath I walk past a young deer that seems entirely unafraid of me, and communicates a greeting through its soft brown eyes. I reciprocate this exchange and continue down the path, my heart filled with joy at this new world.

As I continue to walk I begin to hear a voice calling my name, a voice that is instantly familiar. I turn my head to listen more closely and am taken by surprise as I see my mother running frantically towards me.

'Mother?!' I call out, the comfort of my old life bringing conflicting emotions. For the second time, another person passes straight through me. I turn, and the beautiful valley is gone and I see her running down Elm Tree Lane, screaming my name as I lie motionless on the ground.

***

'Anna!' She drops to the gravel beside me and lifts my head onto her lap, brushing my hair and grit from my face. I see her crying, great sobs of fear as she holds onto me. 'Don't worry, my angel. The ambulance will be here soon. Oh God, help me, I don't know what to do.'

She looks desperately up the lane, willing the ambulance to hurry as I remain unconscious and limp in her arms. I have never seen my mother like this before. She strokes my face and tears fall from her beautiful face onto my ashen cheeks.

'I have loved you since the day you were born, Anna. My strong, wilful girl. I wish I had your strength and had taken you away from him. We could have had a happier life. I am so sorry. Please live and I will make everything right. I promise. I promise.'

The sirens drown out her desolate cries and within moments she is pulled back from me by paramedics, and grasping her trembling hands together she prays for her dying daughter.

'We have a weak pulse.' A young man in his twenties places an oxygen mask over my face and I'm hastily lifted onto a stretcher as my mother tells them what's wrong with me.

'Do you know her medication? What she has taken today?'

As I am placed in the stretcher she jumps in and finds the pill bottles in my bag. 'She takes these three times a day and these twice.' Her hands shake violently as she hands them to the paramedic.

'And these?' He shows her the third bottle of my trusted pain killers.

'They're low dose multivitamins,' my mother tells him, and I am stunned at this revelation. 'She was relying too much on painkillers; they made her worse. I switched them before it got out of hand.'

He raises his eyebrows uncertainly and she looks at him with incredibly steady focus, as though that had been without doubt the right thing to do. I watch the scene play out and I cannot help smiling as I realise no wonder they had stopped taking effect. I feel incredibly confused at seeing her from this new perspective.

The ambulance doors slam shut and the sound

makes me jump, bringing me back to the present and the only thing before me is a winding lane I feel compelled to follow.

CHAPTER SEVEN:

BEAUTY AND THE BEASTS

I had not seen my Great Grandmother for almost five years but I knew the figure standing in front of the pretty cottage immediately. She only came clearly into focus as I ran further down the lane, and became flooded with memories of running towards her as young girl.

I stop abruptly as I look properly at her, remembering that for the last few years of her life she had fought bravely with my own nemesis. When I had kissed her cheek for the last time as she lay dying, her skin had been ghostly white and red rings circled her lined eyes. The body of the woman, who had once lifted us high into the air, could not have lifted a feather. She had been skeletal, a shell whose inhabitant had abandoned her long ago.

'Grandma?' I ask uncertainly, as the woman before me does not look old at all.

'Darling, come here!' She laughs joyfully and I fall into her arms, assured once more it is her. I step back and see she looks about forty, an age I don't remember knowing her, and she is completely lovely. Bethany's hair is chestnut like Izzy's and long past her shoulders. She looks very similar to my mother with cat-like eyes in a heart-shaped face. They light and twinkle with laughter, as I recall they always had, and they look as though someone has taken Lillian's eyes and turned the dimmer switch up to its brightest.

'Let me look at you,' she tells me, and smiles as she holds my face in her hands. 'Anna, you are just the same.'

'I thought I would never see you again.' I remember how much I had cried after her passing, knowing she had gone for ever.

'You knew you would see me one day, darling, you just didn't *know* that you knew!'

She laughs her tinkling laugh again and beckons me to follow her into the cottage.

Although my heart is filled with joy, I shudder with apprehension as I do not see the dark wolf but I feel his ominous presence nearby.

***

I walk into a room and call out to my Great Grandmother, but she does not respond and unaware of me, continues to carry her tray into the living room. I once again become an unwitting observer to the scene.

A girl of perhaps twelve is crying softly, holding her head in her hands as she sits in a comfortable-looking armchair adorned with crocheted blankets. She is stroking a shaggy dog who sits contentedly in her lap.

'Lillian, my dear. I'm pleased to see you after all this time, but I'll have to tell your parents you're here. They called this morning, and I hope they call again so I can put an end to their worrying. Why on earth have you run away this time?'

'Why have I run away? A thousand reasons! How about because we're moving again? I've only just made friends and wanted to go to their school, I never learn anything in that stupid caravan. Mother doesn't know about anything I want to be taught! I am tired of seeing them get drunk! The men they think are their friends look at me for too long and try to tickle me until I scream and everyone thinks it's funny! I don't want their filthy rough hands anywhere near me.'

She looks gravely concerned and stares hard into the open fire, as though the answer may be found somewhere in the crackling flames.

'They're travellers, darling; they never stay somewhere long enough for you to be in school. I know you get tired of moving but they love you very much. You are a family and you must stay together. You may not like their choice of friends, but I know neither of them would let you come to any harm.'

My young mother snorts and I can tell those words sound as hollow to her ears as they do to mine. I am shocked that my grandparents could have let her be exposed her to this. I begin to feel uncomfortable as I remember the night I drank some of their 'special juice'.

'Grandma, they were so drunk last night they didn't even hear me sneak out. I want to live with you, I hate that pokey caravan. I cannot wait until I am old enough to buy my own house … it'll be big and beautiful and I will stay there for ever!'

I see my Great Grandmother smile sadly as she hands my mother the tray and watches her devour the scones, giving the dog a few crumbs to nibble. It surprises me to see her so fond of the little thing, I could never imagine her, in her crisp, white linen trousers, letting a dog lick sticky jam from her fingers.

A ringing breaks through my reverie and I see Beth run towards an old fashioned phone and lift the receiver. My mother looks horrified as she tells the caller that yes, Lilly is safe and with her. She asks them to call back later tonight when she has had time to think.

'Lilly, they are terribly worried. You must stop running away, that is not the answer. I think you should stay here with me for now, at least until I know what to do.' My mother laughs happily as the little dog licks her face and she looks pleased to discover her determination may have won at last. I cannot help but think that she looks remarkably like me.

***

I'm being guided towards another room and as the door opens I see a busy street, and my mother (a little older) is apologising to a handsome man as she picks up his books from the pavement.

'I'm so sorry, I didn't see you!' She picks up the last book and smiles at him before hurrying into a room past a sign saying, 'Auction.'

The man is without a doubt my father, but I am taken aback by how young and good looking he is. He's in his twenties and still has very dark hair and a moustache, but it is trimmed neatly. His hair is gelled fashionably into place. With a bemused look on his face he follows her past the sign and finds her looking at a tired and tattered-looking sofa.

She smiles when she sees him. 'I need furniture for my flat. I'm going to university to study History.'

'How old are you?' he asks, unable to take his eyes off her face.

'Nineteen.' I see her flick her hair over her shoulders the way I used to and I realise she likes him. I understand that he must seem very impressive to her considering her upbringing. He's dressed in an expensive grey suit and has an imposing aura. People were noticing him amongst the tatter and jumble and I could sense that my mother appreciated that. Perhaps she saw an opportunity for the life she had always dreamed of, a proper family living in a big house with a garden where she could live for ever. In that instant, maybe the smell of the dingy caravan of her youth became a little less prevalent. I understood her a little better as she smiled at this man, a radiant beautiful smile that clearly beguiled him. He asked her name, and I noted that she almost said 'Lilly,' then quickly changed to telling him 'Lillian.'

***

Vibrations intensify as the scene vanishes and I walk down a dark corridor of what seems to be a hotel. I push open the nearest door and recoil as I see him on top of my mother.

The room is shrouded in darkness, but a low glow from a brass lamp casts shadows. I avert my eyes from where they lie on the grand bed, and see a wedding dress discarded on the dusty floor, its beautiful silk layers crumpled and creased and smudged with dirt. An almost full bottle of champagne stands on a circular table aside two crystal glasses, and the bubbles still dance a little around the rims, untouched and untasted.

I hear her whimpering and cannot stop myself from looking back to her. His hand is pressed firmly over her mouth and tears fall silently from her once radiant eyes as he pounds roughly inside her.

I wonder why I am being shown this untrue vision. My father would never behave this way. He gives a final painful thrust, stifling her scream and pulls quickly away from her, a look of distaste on his handsome face, as he wipes her tears and coral lipstick from his hand.

'Well?' he says as he straightens the clothes he hadn't bothered to take off. 'Was it worth making me wait till we were married?' He laughs nastily and continues, 'Don't fuss like that every time, you'll have to become accustomed if we're to have a child.'

My mother says nothing but has pulled the blanket up over her breasts with trembling hands. He looks at her with a cold stare. 'You'll get used to it, I'm sure, unless you want to go back to your little caravan?' He laughs. 'Get dressed. I need cigarettes then I'll take you for dinner.'

'Children?' she whispers, her eyes widened with shock. 'I'm only nineteen. I haven't finished my studies, Malcolm.'

He steps towards her and she pulls the blanket up further in haste. 'You're my *wife*, Lillian, not a damn student – A wife who will take care of my home and give me a family to come home to – Isn't that what you wanted? When I showed you Elm Tree and you danced and sang and told me how our beautiful children would play in the meadow? How we would be so happy. You said you wanted that, are you to break your promises after a few hours of marriage? Shall I send you back to Granny with no money and no Elm Tree?'

I can see my mother is still in shock, that the man who probably smiled down at her a matter of hours ago as he said his vows, who had offered her the life she had dreamed of as a child, turned suddenly into this tyrant.

'I do want to have a family one day ...'

'What you want,' he interrupts her loudly, making me jump, 'is of no great consequence, Lillian. You are married. For God's sake get dressed, and sort yourself out. You look like a slut.' He curls his lip in disgust and she flinches involuntarily. 'I want your hair tied up from now on, and we'll get you some decent clothes. You need to look *and* act like the wife of a successful merchant. Things are going to be a lot be different if this is to work.'

He straightens his moustache in the dingy mirror and leaves the room, the slamming door making her start.

I cry with her as she swings her legs over the bed, walking unsteadily to the dressing table, and I flinch at the sight of blood on her pale thighs. She reaches for a silver-backed paddle brush and scrapes her beautiful long hair into the familiar chignon she wore the last time I saw her.

'Oh, Mother,' I whisper, and her frightened face

turns towards me, but her glassy eyes do not meet mine. She is alone.

***

My legs are trembling a little and I cannot process what I've just seen. The corridors open and close around me and I feel as though I am in Wonderland once more as I feel myself falling through a vast nothingness, lost and afraid.

I jolt to a halt and see that I'm now standing in our hallway at Elm Tree; I know my parents have lived there since they were first married, so I'm not surprised to see my mother sitting on the bottom steps of the grand stair case, her hands clasped in prayer and a suitcase beside her. Her body is thinner than the Lillian I saw moments ago on her wedding night, and her face is drawn and pale. Perhaps only a year has passed, because she still looks incredibly young. Vulnerable and afraid, on the stairs of the home she had dreamed of. She looks dishevelled, and her hair is falling from its clasps.

My father runs down each step two at a time and as she jumps up and begins to run forwards, he grabs her trailing hair so her neck jolts painfully back.

I try to close my eyes or turn my head but my entire being is frozen as I watch him spin her around and punch her in the mouth. Blood pours from the gash and her face is distorted. 'Just kill me!' she screams at him. 'I have nothing to live for. I've lost my baby because of you!'

My father lets go of her and his face turns ghostly white. 'What?'

'I was pregnant, Malcolm. When you thought I was sneaking off to see someone I was going to the doctors. I wanted to be certain before I told you.'

'Then why didn't you tell me, Lillian? I thought you were acting differently. I thought you were going to leave me.' He begins to sob uncontrollably and drops to the floor. 'Please forgive me, my love. That's all I've ever wanted for us. A family to fill this big house, to keep you busy when I'm not here with you. A boy ...' He chokes on the word and brings his hands to his face. My mother curls her broken lip as he blows his streaming nose into his fist. 'A strong boy, to carry on my name.'

He looks at her with more urgency and takes a moment to compose himself. 'You can't leave me; we have to put this right. It can't be my fault, I barely touched you. If you didn't do such stupid things and make me angry ...' His eyes open wider. 'We'll try again and this time it'll be perfect. I'll never hurt you, I promise. We'll be the family we dreamed of.'

My mother shakes her head sadly, and as he grabs her arm his tone turns swiftly from pleading to anger. 'If you leave me, you will leave with nothing. You have nowhere to go, you have no friends, or do you want to go back to the family you've all but abandoned? You can say goodbye to your designer clothes and your precious antiques. Are you really ready to leave Elm Tree for ever? To give up on your dream and go back to drifting from one filthy place to the next?'

My mother looks uncertain and afraid. I have always sensed weakness from her, but I am certain she will find the strength somewhere to leave after all he has done.

To my horror, she picks up the heavy suitcase at her feet and carries it past him, back up the sweeping staircase as he smooths down his hair with both hands.

I stay close to her for a little while, trying to offer some comfort but of course she doesn't know I am there. A little while later she walks silently out into the garden, looking behind her to see if he is watching. Held out carefully in front of her is a small plant cupped gently between her hands, and she moves quickly to the secluded rose garden behind the elm tree. I watch her embed the plant amongst the pungent soils with such tenderness I that I am quite moved.

'You were not a boy to carry on his name, darling. You were a little girl to live your life full of dreams and laughter. You would have always remembered how to laugh as I have forgotten. I would have raised you in this beautiful house, and given you everything I never had. I shall never forget you or stop loving you and I hope there are angels who will protect you where I failed.'

I am left lost and alone, wondering if it meant that somewhere in this afterlife, Izzy and I have a sister who was lost before birth. My anger towards Father is boundless. I run towards the house but as the door swings open, everything is different as though many years have passed, and I see my mother pulling us up the stairs and telling us to hurry. She gently ushers Izzy and I into the attic room, full of toys and wall hangings, and tells us to play quietly. I see her lock the door and run back down the stairs as my father storms up the driveway and into the house.

'Where are they?' he bellows. 'Have you seen what they have done to the garden?! I have people coming for dinner in an hour and it looks like a jumble sale out there!'

'Malcolm, please. Calm down, I have time to clear it up. They were having such a nice time playing tea parties. I have everything ready for tonight ...' Her voice trails away and she lifts her hand in a practised motion to defend her face from the imminent blow.

'Do you want to leave?' He spits each word as she picks herself up from the floor, eyeing him wearily. I see that the radiant face which had looked up at him all those years ago had been replaced with a stone mask. Her eyes were dead as she told him, no, she didn't want to leave.

'Because you know what will happen, don't you, Lillian?' She nods silently. '*You* will be the one to leave but *my* girls will stay here. Without you guarding them like a she-wolf I could show them proper discipline.' His laugh is so ugly that I shudder. He smiles nastily. 'No. I don't think you'll be leaving yet. Not just yet.'

I cannot stand there listening any more and run down the lane from Elm Tree praying that this will stop; praying that this was a mistake and my father couldn't possibly be such a monster. 'I would have known!' I scream into the darkness. 'I would have known.' I fall to my knees and let the cold air wash over me, wondering how anything could ever be good again.

Chapter Eight:

THE ONE YOU FEED

'Sit still on the carpet, Anna!' I am surprised to hear the exasperated sound of my alternative Sunday school teacher, Mr Thomas. He looks exactly how I remember him; the dog collar worn over a tie-dyed T shirt, strange harem trousers, and open-toed sandals. His long hair is neatly pulled into a ponytail, and his blue eyes are sparkling with mischief.

As I look around I am sitting in a neat circle with my peers while he stands at the front of the room. Rather than looking straight through me in the fashion to which I am now accustomed, he is staring right at me so I quickly cross my legs and realise that I am a little girl once more as I look at my shiny, patent leather shoes.

'So.' He seems satisfied and gets back to his story. 'We all have two wolves fighting inside us. A good wolf and a bad wolf ... and the battle is ferocious!' He says the last part with great enthusiasm and we all giggle.

'What, little ones, do we think the good wolf might be fighting for?' He had told us this popular old fable many times and a few of the boys piped up.

'Courage! Mr Thomas! And love, and kindness!'

'Excellent, you have remembered so well! What else might he be fighting for? Anna, can you think of something good worth fighting for?'

I was tempted to say Cadbury's Creme Eggs but I am enjoying this happy memory of a simpler time, so I shout out eagerly, 'Honesty and happiness and hope, Mr Thomas!'

He chuckles, then his face darkens and our eyes pop like saucers. 'But what, children, do we think the *baaaad* wolf inside you is fighting for?'

We must all be looking a little *too* disconcerted because he stops snarling quite so aggressively and raises his eyebrows for an answer.

'Greed!' shouts a brave soul to the left of me, inspiring us all to join in.

'And hatred and jealousy and evil!'

Mr Thomas claps his hands as the church bells ring, indicating we can join our parents now their sermons are over. As we run out, he calls after us, 'Remember, my little fledglings; the wolf that wins is the one that you feed!'

None of us hear him, and as I look back through

my seventeen-year-old eyes, I wonder if perhaps he does look a little stoned.

***

I walk out of the church and sense that I have returned to my present state. I feel a little calmer for the happy reverie, and a bird singing beautifully restores my faith that perhaps I can find some peace here. I desperately miss Michael, and I need to find a way to tell my mother that I'm sorry for being such a terrible daughter, now I knew she had sacrificed her life to give us things she never had. I never would have wanted that. How could she have loved Elm Tree so much? It would have made more sense to me had she hated her beautiful prison.

If I had ever known of her silent anguish I would have told her to leave him. Why did she not run away like she used to when she was twelve? Perhaps it was through fear for our safety if she left us with him, or at his anger if she had tried to take us with her. I sigh sadly and wonder how such things could have happened without us knowing. No wonder Elm Tree was so lifeless, another beautiful shell with no soul.

As I walk by myself down the wandering lanes, I start to recall wisps of memories from my younger years. Turning music up loud so Izzy could not hear him shouting at her, drinking vodka at sixteen when I realised it helped to forget. Had I really buried so much without knowing? I feel a great heaviness surrounding me as I understand there is nothing I can do for her now. And the cold hand of fear grips my heart once more as I remember she is with him still and I have left her behind.

***

The sky darkens in keeping with my mood and the shimmering dark wolf suddenly emerges at my side, beckoning me to follow him to what appears to be a derelict building. He leaves me to tread carefully through the bricks and debris and as I see more similar ruins ahead, I sense that I am walking through the ghost of a town that has been torn apart by war. The buildings that remain have had their insides blown out, leaving shards and shatters of glass beneath my feet.

'Is anyone here?' I call out, feeling more destitute than ever.

My voice breaks into a lonely echo and I shiver in the dust and decay. I close my eyes and try to imagine the comfort of home, but all I see is the lie I have lived. My parent's discord, my mother's quest to suffer in silence as her two spoiled girls laughed and sang, oblivious. I dispel the dark thoughts and search my soul for a memory of Michael to save me. My heart lifts as I see his face, then disintegrates as the image vanishes and I know that he belongs to another world.

The only angel watching over me now is dark and of despair, and had I encompassed the power to end the anguish, I would have done so now without a moment's hesitation.

A noise at my feet brings my head reluctantly up from my knees, and I see an emerging black beetle tunnelling upwards from the dust and dry earth. I watch him for a few moments busying around in the decay, and instantly feel a little better that I am not the only one sent to this dire place. I watch, fascinated, as he comes closer to me, making a slow but persistent trail to the stack of rubble I have lain against. I cannot help but think that although he is my only companion, I have never liked bugs and find him rather ugly.

Vibrations pick up between us and I am embarrassed to find that he may have read my mind.

'I am Hope,' he tells me and I look at him dubiously.

'There is hope here?' I ask him.

'Of course,' he replies, scuttling away from me now with more purpose than ever, 'Where there is life, Anna, there is Hope.'

I feel he may have been laughing at me, yet I cannot help but smile as I realise it is time for me to progress, and I thank the little beetle before turning in the opposite direction. As we move further away from each other and our vibrations begin to weaken, I am certain I feel him whisper, 'Remember me.'

***

I walk in solitude before noticing a remarkably tall man ahead of me, wearing a white linen suit and a Panama hat.

'Anna! At last, my goodness, I have been waiting for you!' I like him immediately and run shyly towards him, falling alongside his meandering pace. 'Well, what do you think of it here? Like it?' His British accent is very old-fashioned and although he is no longer made up of dazzling lights, I recognise him as my Guide.

'No!' I cry out to him. 'I do not like what I've seen!'

'Did you not like to see Benji and Maria?'

'Well, yes. That part was nice.'

'And your Great Grandmother?'

I turn to face him so he will understand the seriousness of how distraught I am.

'Yes! Of course I wanted to see her but she showed me terrible things. My mother ...' My voice trails away and he pats my shoulder gently.

'Anna, did you not need to know why your mother was so sad? Are you not glad that you can see how much she loved you? She sacrificed her happiness so you could grow up in a beautiful house, and have the stability she never had.'

'I didn't need any of that! She should have left

him and we would have had a proper chance to be happy.' I cry silently and his strident voice startles me.

'Anna, you have so much to learn. Come and sit with me.' A fallen log offers its service.

'I have watched over you for many years, and see the way you are all too willing to let negative influences in. It is almost as though you are drawn to self-destructive emotion.'

I frown crossly as he continues. 'You've had countless opportunity to live at a higher level, and yet you always bury your head in the sand with your silly outlets.'

I look at his irritatingly serene expression, my features so scrunched up in annoyance that my face turns pink.

'Anna, you look displeased. Can you not agree that for all your mother was desperately unhappy, her sacrifices blessed you with many fortuitous options? She took your father's temper away from you and Isabel. You were safe and loved, attended the best schools, dance classes, birthday parties ... so why were you such an unsatisfied little thing?'

I think for a moment and tell him, 'I can remember being happy. Before Izzy was born and I was still little, my mother and I spent a lot of time together and I'm sure I was happy.'

I close my eyes and consciously allow him to share a memory of my mother and I visiting a beautiful estate in Buckingham. The rambling old manor had housed noble families and entertained visiting kings and queens from as far back as the grandiose Tudor Courtiers. I loved her telling me stories of King Henry as he had slept in a certain room while guards stood by the heavy panelled doors of his chambers. She told me he wanted sons as heirs to his throne, and how wicked he was to his queens when they delivered only baby girls. There were various artefacts from each era and I had breathed excitedly over every display cabinet, my eyes wide as she told me intriguing stories of people that sounded to me more like fairy tale characters.

A ruthless king beheading his queen, young princes locked in towers, and armies fighting for titles and power. She told me of a beautiful Scottish princess, born into great power and becoming Queen at just six days old, and showed me her portrait as a young woman fighting to keep her country from the grasp of men. I remember my mother's face in great detail, how beautiful and animated it was as she spoke of how women had to be brave.

Bending down. I watched her avidly as she held onto my shoulders and told me to listen. 'Never let someone rule over you, Anna. You must always be brave and strong. Stand up for yourself and what you believe in.'

I nodded furiously, thinking she was just like

the beautiful queens and princesses of her stories.

My memory is so vivid I am taken away on the strength of its recollection. I am holding my mother's hand as we walk happily towards the car. She is singing to me a nursery rhyme and I skip along enjoying the sun on my face.

As she fastens her seatbelt, I see she is heavily pregnant, and find I am an observer once more, no longer a participant of the pretty scene before me. We sing all the way along the winding roads until I stop abruptly and tell her I need ice cream.

'Darling, we don't have time for ice cream. I told your father we would be back in the house by four and it is almost quarter past five. I have to prepare dinner.'

I recognise the scrunched up face of disappointment, and even I see myself as spoilt when my bottom lip begins to tremble.

'Oh. All right, Anna. I'll stop at the next village and see if we can find some.' She laughs as my face transforms into a cheerful grin and pats her tummy. 'Perhaps your little brother or sister would like some too.'

Before we reach the village, Lillian sees an ice cream van with a small queue in the car park of a country pub. 'Perfect,' she says, and pulls in quickly, telling me to wait in the car as she pulls alongside it.

I must have forgotten what happens next but as she returns with two ice cream cones, my mother's smiling face turns to confusion as her eyes fall upon a man and a much younger brunette kissing and laughing together at a table in the beer garden. She stands still for only a moment then runs to the car, dropping her dessert on the ground, and almost throwing mine at me. As she hastily pulls on her seat belt and starts the engine I see myself ask her, 'What's wrong, Mummy?' Then my little worried face turns to look to see my father running towards us as she screeches away.

Despite my mother's attempts at reassurance, I sit quietly for the journey, as children do when they sense something is wrong. She detours from Elm Tree to my grandparents' house and leaves me there crying and begging to go home with her.

'I have to go to the shops for more ice cream, darling,' she tells me, but I do not want more ice cream and her lie is too transparent for my sharp senses. 'Be good for Grandma and I will be back soon.'

I am ushered into the living room while my Grandma runs after her as she heads back to the car. 'Lilly, whatever is wrong, dear? You shouldn't be so worked up, the baby is due in a few weeks. Come in and have a cool drink. I'm worried about you.'

My mother just pulls away and says, 'It is true. I have seen it with my own eyes today. So much for a new baby and a new beginning, I am such a hypocrite telling Anna to be brave and strong when

I can't even walk away from a man who treats me this way. Why do I give him this power?' She sounds bewildered, as if this is happening to somebody else and is beyond her comprehension. My grandma reaches for her once more, but Lillian pulls away the way I have seen myself do to her.

'I will leave this time, Mother. I have been hiding some money. I will get things for the baby and Anna's clothes, then I will be back. I am going to take them as far away from him as I can.' She suddenly smiles and I find myself crying at the hope in her beautiful face. 'I can do this – for them. I won't be afraid of him any more.'

The next time I saw my mother was nine days later. She brought Izzy home from hospital, her face bruised and her arm broken.

***

Love radiates from my Guide and I rest my head on his shoulders. 'I don't remember Father being so mean,' I say quietly.

He nods and rests his head against mine. 'She protected you, but all of those vibrations around you were so inharmonious, you picked up much negativity and carried it with you. By the time Isabel was born, your parents had settled into quiet discontentment. She turned a blind eye to his affairs and tried to avoid his temper at all costs. Your sister did not suffer the same tumultuous vibrations that you did.'

'Is that why she is so happy and I'm not?'

He paused for a second, treading carefully. 'Isabel is of a different nature, she has less of a journey to travel than you do, Anna. She is no more or less good, just at a different stage in her development.'

I try to read between the lines as he smiles and continues, 'Every soul will progress to exactly the same level. We will all reach a point when we become one with our Higher Self. In that state we are enlightened and fully evolved. It usually happens over a number of lifetimes, within each one learning new attributes and progressing further. It is up to each of us how far we travel. Of course, the faster we learn to live with joy, the faster we become our Higher Selves. The road is more difficult for some, but that does not make it less extraordinary or beautiful or worthwhile. Some people experience extreme grief, or have to live through turbulent years, and face illness or disability. Just try to remember that our journeys may be very different but our destinations are all the same.' He gives a satisfied nod while I am left angry and confused.

He stands up to leave me, removing the Panama hat and smoothing down his white hair.

'Isabel is equal to you, as we all are to each other, but she has progressed further than you at this time. She has learned contentment over her evolvement; she is peaceful and has faith in others.

It may have taken her time to find tranquillity but it will come to us all eventually.' He looks at me with sparkling eyes. 'It will come to you too. You will find a time in your life when you learn to love unconditionally. Your anger will simply dissipate and you will be quite selfless.' His mouth twitches into a smile at his last drop of wisdom.

I look at him wryly, hating to point out the obvious. 'Not in *this* lifetime, though. I might come back as Mother-bloody-Teresa in the next one but for now, Anna Winters in all her messed up glory, is left for dead on an operating table. I can't go back and save my mother from her misery, I can't learn to love my sister without envy, I can't do good things for other people ...' My voice trails away as I think of Michael. I won't see the golden horse he spoke about, or be able to love unconditionally as I desperately wanted. 'I won't grow old with him.'

The Guide must have seen enough self-pity, for he smiles and walks away.

Although it should have shocked or surprised me tremendously, I find I am quite undeterred when his body transforms into the white wolf, bowing his head before vanishing.

***

I feel I have been walking for hours before my surroundings become reassuringly familiar. I recognise the lake by which my journey began and run to the shore where Benji is waiting.

'Well?' he asks in greeting.

'I feel a thousand years older, Ben. I've seen the worst and most beautiful sights of my lifetime, and have been left alone to contemplate how it is too late for me put anything right.'

'Oh, Anna you never listen. That is the whole point of progression, you do not stand still. Not ever! Make a decision to either put things right or advance on a different journey. Whatever you decide, you will carry with you a new knowledge. It may sometimes feel like a little voice in your ear, a moment in your conscience, or a feeling in your heart. We are so institutionalised as earth-bound beings we ignore many of these messages, but you must remember to listen to them. Recognise when you are being guided and you will begin to make different choices as you have learned from your old ones. Listen to your inner voice and follow the path of your higher self.'

I look back along the road which brought me here.

'Well?' he laughs, as if the answer is so obvious and in the space of a second, a thousand visions flash before me. I feel my birth, the powerful force of maternal love, and the unending confidence in the intuition we are born with. I feel the confidence ebb and wane as life influences me. I see Izzy as a little girl, running towards me, her eyes full of adoration for her big sister. I am growing. I am making mistakes but I am learning. I am falling in love. I see Michael in the hospital corridor and start running towards his image at great speed, with all the determined power of my human body I am hurtling back to him.

Back to my family.

My heart is lifted with the highest joy. I know with certainty that I can return to my life. My wild and foolish, heart-achingly wonderful life.

PART THREE

PART THREE

Chapter Nine:

WHERE WE ARE

A loud beeping begins to pierce my subconscious and I hear frantic voices around me asking me to open my eyes. I choke painfully as a long tube is pulled from my throat, and I feel as though I am being whisked away from a dream before I am ready to awaken. My last thought before the pain kicks in is of a girl I used to know. I am being pulled further and faster away from her as she calls out to me desperately. Her voice is carried away on the faintest breeze as I draw a deep breath into my lungs.

'Save Marley for me, Anna.' Then her beautiful aquamarine eyes are gone.

My next breath is equally painful and I fight the urge to throw up, fearing I may choke as a nurse tells me in what is presumably her most soothing voice to try and breathe normally. If I could have felt my arms I would have grabbed her, but I can only lie motionless with each shuddering breath.

A familiar voice enters the room and I hear Mr Raj tell me to open my eyes. I am reassured by his presence, but my efforts are rewarded with an excruciating beam of light into my left pupil. Utterly enraged, my strength slowly returns, but I am jabbed with a sedative injection before I have the chance to throttle him.

My next awakening is a little less painful, and I open my eyes to see three worried faces: Izzy, Michael, and my mother. I smile at Izzy, offer Michael a look of pure love, and frown crossly at Lillian. They stare back at me before my eyes close and sleep steals me away.

I dream of uncertain creatures, animals that change form from beast to human. I hope I am dreaming as I hear Izzy telling me she has borrowed my Patrick Cox ballet pumps. My eyes squint open a painful crack as she laughs and tells me, 'Ha! I knew you were listening!' She presses the nurse call button by my bed. 'Don't get your knickers in a twist; I can't find where you've hidden them.'

I cannot speak but I can smile inwardly. When I found out I had cancer I hid my favourite shoes in the attic so she would *never* get her hands on them if I ever did kick the bucket.

I open my eyes again, feeling incredibly unsure of what was happening to me. The tube was thankfully removed from my throat and my head pounded.

'Anna!' My mother comes rushing into the room and holds my hand, planting a gentle kiss on my forehead.

There is a little bit of commotion as two nurses fuss round me, and the next person I see is Mr Raj.

'Well, Miss Winters,' he smiles proudly. 'Did I not tell you that you were in safe hands?' He shines the light in my eyes again and continues his fondness for ridiculous questions.

'Can you tell me your first name?'

'Anna.' I think the word with certainty but they do not reach my mouth. I have not forgotten my name, but I have forgotten how to speak.

'How many fingers?'

I frown as I look up at his hand, but all of his fingers are blurred, and even if I could talk, I could not possibly distinguish one from another.

'Miss Winters, can you blink once if you can hear me.'

I blink to show him I understand and a frightened tear escapes as I slowly open and close my eyes. My mother tightens her grip on my hand just a little. She looks to Mr Raj.

'Don't worry, dear. We are very pleased that you have woken up. We had to keep you heavily sedated after I operated on your tumour. Yesterday we removed sedation and were delighted that you were breathing without support. You will feel very disorientated for a while as your brain and body adjust to normal function, but your CT scan was very promising.' He leans forward and I feel calmer as I can now focus on his kind brown eyes. 'Very promising indeed.'

I hear my mother ask him anxiously, 'She will be all right, won't she? You said everything went well despite her collapse.'

I widen my eyes to signal my alarm and Izzy appears next to them. 'You collapsed at home before they could operate, but the tumour has gone now, Anna. You just need to rest and get better so we can take you home.' Her lovely eyes are full of tears and I am glad she is there. Izzy is always so certain where Mother is questions and constant worry. I do not want to hear the details and held on to Izzy's confident words. 'The tumour has gone.'

Mr Raj continues his examination and I have to blink in response as he checks I have sensation from my head to my feet, more shining light into my pupils and then he retreats with his colleagues, ordering me to rest. I look over to my mother's pale face and try to manage a smile. I am so tired I feel I could sleep for a thousand years until my thoughts turn to one focus, Michael. But the sound is jumbled and comes out in a soft moan. I try again but Mother irritatingly keeps shushing me and tells me to rest. I close my eyes crossly to shut her out, and when I next open them, I am overjoyed to see him beside me.

'Hello, darling.' Despite being half dead I almost leap up at the sound of his voice, and manage what I hope is a pretty smile.

He strokes my head tenderly and offers me a drink from a glass with a straw. 'They say you need to have lots of fluids. I'm going to take care of you.' He helps me sit forward slightly and I sip some water. The icy cold liquid tastes so foreign in my mouth but soothes my throat beautifully. I take big gulps for Michael, wanting him to take care of me. I lie back against the pillows and wished I was wearing lip gloss.

He smiles at me and says, 'Do you remember when I'd had my operation?' I nod happily, remembering falling in love. 'I woke up so confused I thought you were a nurse till I saw your headscarf. You wouldn't leave me alone, making sure I ate and drank and did my exercises.' I smile again as he tells me it is his time for revenge.

'I won't let an hour go by without fussing about with protein shakes and orange segments!' He leans forward and kisses my brow. 'I have to go and fetch your mother; she made me promise to as soon as you woke up.' I frown and try to tell him not to be crazy, I am happier when it is just the two of us, but he is up and rushing excitedly out of the door before my lips whisper one tiny sound, 'Michael.'

After initial concern regarding my speech, Mr Raj is regretting his competent success, as by week two I am shouting at him once more.

'I look like bloody Frankenstein!' The hand mirror shows ugly criss-cross stitches across the left side of my head.

'Anna!' My mother sounds suitably shocked. 'Do not speak to the doctor like that after all he has done for you.' She shakes her head crossly and I look like I may kill her as she goes on to say, 'And Frankenstein was the creator, not the monster!'

Michael thankfully steps between us and tries to calm me as I have been raging for an hour. He wipes tears from my eyes with his thumbs. 'Your hair will cover the scar in no time. Remember that your chemo and radio are done, angel, and your hair will grow back quickly so no one will ever know there was a scar there at all.'

His soothing voice works. He has never called me 'angel' before, which I rather like. Although I avoid Izzy's eyes as I know they will be dubious at his term of endearment.

I slam down the mirror on the table in front of me and let out a dramatic sigh as my mother replaces my favoured head scarf from Dr. Braby. I cannot wear a wig until the swelling and scarring has healed.

'There,' she says as I smack her fussing hands away. 'Do you want me to take you to Physio or should Michael do it?'

I roll my eyes and beckon Michael to bring over the wheelchair. Despite the operation being a success, I have a long road ahead of me, and although my speech came back quickly, I have to learn to walk again gradually. I hated the stupid wheelchair and only allowed Michael to push it. Izzy refused after I insisted on wearing a sheet over my head the first time I had to be wheeled to the Physio department, as I was too mortified to be seen.

'You realise you look like a bloody ghost?' she had shouted at me last week. 'How can I push you around like that without dying of humiliation?'

The disabled ghost had sat silently and stolidly until her sister had continued wheeling her to the lifts, burning with embarrassment and muttering, 'Never again.'

I had since been coaxed out of the sheet but still frowned with my chin tucked into my chest as Michael laughed and wheeled me down the never-ending corridors.

CHAPTER TEN:

A STEP TOO FAR

Lillian is humming softly as we drive the winding roads to Elm Tree. I look out of the window at the picture perfect snow, settling softly on the pine trees that line the country lanes, then turn to my mother.

'What's that song?' I ask, thinking I might like it.

'It's not a song, darling, it is Chopin.' I roll my eyes and look at her suspiciously. Is there an air of victory about her as she carefully manoeuvres the bend in the road that leads to our driveway?

Yesterday, I was gleefully packing my belongings with Izzy and Michael, as Mr Raj had granted me the all clear to go home. I had been pestering him for days to be free of the stifling hospital, and finally (with a little persuasion from Dr. Braby) he had conceded to my discharge in time for Christmas.

Michael looked at me shyly and asked if I wanted to spend Christmas at the ranch with him. I had yet to meet his father and step-mother; I hadn't wanted to be introduced until I felt I looked more respectable and was feeling better.

I saw Lillian catch her breath and heard Izzy's heart stop beating. I knew they would go along with anything I wanted, but I also knew they were desperate to take care of me themselves. I had even been getting along reasonably well with my mother of late.

I smiled at Michael and thanked him. 'I would love to, but I can't expect these two to manage Christmas without me. *She* …' I gesture my thumb behind me towards Izzy, 'couldn't decorate a tree if her life depended on it. And *she* …' I point at my worried-looking mother, 'can hardly cook a baked bean never mind a turkey!'

They both clapped their hands delightedly and Izzy ran up behind me with a big bear hug. 'Anna, we'll have the best Christmas ever!' I caught my mother's eye and we shared a rare and loving smile.

So perhaps this was the reason she still seemed rather pleased as the familiar crunch of gravel announced our arrival onto Elm Tree Lane.

I could have cried with happiness as I saw the fairy lights twinkling in our namesake tree. The dusk had crept upon us quickly, just in time to showcase the starry lights. I saw the front of the house was also lit with Christmas decorations and guessed it was for my benefit, as never before had home looked so welcomingly festive.

'I love it!' I cry out, and am out of the car before it's barely stopped moving. Izzy is hot on my heels and boasts proudly that they had spent most of the night making sure everything was perfect. I uncharacteristically love Christmas, and it's one of the only occasions where my father and I ever conflict. He cannot abide what he describes as 'gaudy tributes to a misplaced tradition,' and always made us stick to wreaths of holly and a solitary pine in the corner of the entrance hall. He was usually quite generous with his gifts (or at least Leona was), but there was never any tinsel to admire or glittery crackers to pull.

I laugh delightedly as I see the twinkling reindeer by the front door, and spin round to look at my mother. 'Father will go crazy! He'll tear it down as soon as he lays eyes on it.' I stand protectively by Rudolph.

'Oh, leave him to me, Anna. I want this Christmas to be extra special. Anyway, Scrooge won't be home until the twenty-third so we have three days to enjoy it by ourselves.'

My jaw drops involuntarily as she calls him 'Scrooge.' Izzy and I look at each other and while we carry my bags through the front door the three of us twitter and giggle like schoolgirls.

'Oh … my … goodness.' I turn in awestruck circles at the transformation of Elm Tree House. The tree in the entrance hall almost touches the ceiling and is covered with tinsel, baubles, cherubs, and snowflakes. I reach out with delight and touch the wrapped chocolates and candy canes. As I run through the house, every room is decorated beautifully with mistletoe, holly, and scented candles that remind me of the cinnamon mulled wine Grandma Beth used to make. We dance around, singing, jumping from one Christmas carol to another, until my mother claps her hands and orders us to rest on the sofa as she lights the fire. She heats some mulled wine and fresh mince pies with huge dollops of brandy cream and I sigh contentedly. I can't remember ever feeling so happy.

***

Despite the fact I won't see Michael until he comes to visit on Boxing Day, my euphoria continues to glow right up until Christmas Eve. My father had been delayed so it is with a little trepidation that Izzy and I wait for him in the kitchen, sipping a Baileys for Dutch courage.

'Izzy, do you think he'll be mad?'

My sister nods her head. 'Considering the house looks like Santa's Grotto meets Las Vegas, then yes, I'm quite sure he will be furious.'

As if on cue, we hear the crunch of gravel as

Father's Land Rover pulls up in front of the house. It is quarter past five so he will have already seen the outside illuminations in all their splendour. He looks suitably perplexed as he steps into the overwhelmingly festive entrance hall. I walk towards him and to my delight he opens his arms for me to fall in to.

'I'm so sorry, darling, I couldn't be home sooner. I've been worried sick, calling the house every five minutes but your mother never answered.'

Izzy pipes up behind me, 'We were barely ever here, Father. We were at Anna's bedside.'

I turn to look at her crossly. I do not want her to spoil things by trying to make him feel more guilt for not being here sooner. She had said on more than one occasion, 'Surely he could have gotten home by now?' Now she just raises her eyebrows at me and heads back to the kitchen.

'I'm so glad you're home, Father. Do you like my surprise from Mother and Isabel?' I ask him this innocently, gesturing towards the tree and the fairly lights.

'Not my style at all, Annabel,' he says tersely. 'But who cares about all that as long as you are home and well?' He lifts my chin and smiles warmly, until the moment is entirely ruined as the motion-activated Santa suddenly starts singing and wiggling his ample hips. My father visibly stiffens and heads for the drinks cabinet as I curse myself inwardly. Izzy had warned me the singing Santa was a step too far.

***

He disappears upstairs to unpack as Izzy and I breathe a sigh of relief. At least the decorations have not been ordered down. Mother does not look as confident when she arrives home a little while later with shopping.

'He's home then?' she asks nervously, shooing our prying eyes away from the parcels.

'He was fine about it,' I say smugly, as though there was never any doubt. 'All he cared about was that *I* was OK, so as usual you have been fussing and fretting over nothing.'

I manage to grab a Terry's Chocolate Orange from the top of an open carrier bag before she has time to swipe them away. I throw it to Izzy and we run back to the kitchen, leaving Mother to head upstairs with her shopping.

Father comes back downstairs first, freshly showered, with rather glassy eyes from his generous whiskeys. He sits in front of the fire as I fetch him another.

'Does Mother want a drink with us?' Izzy asks as she pours me another miniscule Baileys, rationing my alcohol consumption as subtly as she dare.

'She will, most likely, but I think she's had

enough.' I must look confused as he goes on, 'Had a few glasses of champagne while shopping, by the looks of her. She's only gone and slipped in the bath and hurt herself.'

Izzy jumps up but he motions her to sit still, and I feel further perplexed because she looked fine, and would *never* drink then drive.

I pat my father's arm reassuringly, 'Christmas does funny things to people, and she might have found the shopping centre too manic and needed a little refreshment.'

Izzy looks concerned and I frown at her, silently willing her once more not to make a fuss and spoil Christmas Eve now we were finally all together.

Lillian comes into the room shortly after, dressed in a cream robe and her hair wrapped up in a matching towel. Izzy and I both gasp at her face and despite our father's glares, rush over to her.

'God, Mother, you'll have a black eye for Christmas Day!' I reach out to touch the already discoloured shading around her eye as she flinches away. 'Why have you tried putting makeup over it? We already know you've gotten yourself pissed and slipped over!' I revel in the chance at telling her off for such reckless behaviour and Izzy cannot resist either.

'You've split your lip! Mother, what on earth were you thinking, drinking through the day?'

She looks over at my father as he stands up to lead her to the sofa in a caring manner. 'Leave her alone, girls. I'm sure she feels quite ridiculous enough. I told them you'd a few champagnes while shopping. Won't be repeating that again for a while, eh?'

My mother says nothing as he pours her a brandy. 'Get that down you for the shock.' Izzy and I laugh as he does an impression of her staggering around drunk, while my mother stares straight into the fire, her cheeks burning with embarrassment.

***

I enjoyed Christmas Day but as usual Lillian's dour face put a cloud over the festivities. I think she and my father must have argued over her drinking debacle, as she barely spoke during dinner, although she did try to make sure that Izzy and I had fun, and bought us some lovely gifts.

I opened my present from Michael while they all pretended not to watch, and was annoyed with myself for being a little disappointed with the book about American horses. But I didn't dwell on it, and was comforted by the fact that he wanted me to learn about them as I would be visiting his stables in Northampton soon.

I smiled remembering how cross he gets when I call his ranch 'stables', but it seems so strange to have an American-themed facility in such demonstratively English countryside.

I couldn't wait to go with him though; it would

mean countless days, and more importantly nights, in the company of a man I had fallen deeply in love with. The three months we had known each other seemed like millennia, as though there had never been a time when I had not known and loved him. If any other boyfriend had bought me a horse book for Christmas I would have smacked them around the head with it, but not Michael. I sighed happily and hugged my present.

My mother smiled warmly. 'You shall see him tomorrow, darling. I do like that young man; he has been so good for you and was a great comfort to me when you were in hospital.' She jumped as my father dropped one his golf clubs and it crashed to the floor.

'Izzy bought them, Father, but it was *my* idea,' I said, delighted that we had pleased him with his gift.

'Thank you, Annabel, and Izzy. Did you like your presents?'

My sister and I just looked at one another. Leona seemed to be losing track of our ages (and life-threatening illnesses) as this year she had chosen for us a pair of matching neon roller blades.

We both grinned and made happy noises that we loved our gifts; although I was actually overwhelmed by the beautiful Tiffany charm bracelet my mother had bought me. She bought Izzy a locket, which was also lovely, and I appreciated that she never bought us the same gift.

I gave her shoulder a little squeeze as I walk past her, and she looked very happy as I admire the bracelet on my delicate wrist.

***

I barely sleep through the night knowing Michael will be with me in the morning. I can't imagine there is anything more delicious than lying alone in bed wishing your loved one was there with you. My body tingles as I remember his determined kisses and the confidence with which he made love to me. Despite the December chill, I am suddenly incredibly hot and throw back my blankets, knowing I won't sleep. I sit dreamily on my wooden window seat and press my forehead against the cool window.

It is with much surprise that I see my mother in the little rose garden to the right of the meadow. The lights from the elm tree are just enough that I can see her kneeling by one of the little plants that have been lovingly covered from the frost, despite the fact there is still months until they bloom. I squint my eyes. She looks as though she may be praying. I am distracted by a noise on the landing and I hear my father whispering gruffly, 'Lillian?'

I open the door and he looks startled to see me. 'Why aren't you asleep, Anna?' Then he composes himself and adds, 'Have you seen your mother? I woke up and she wasn't there.'

I don't exactly know why I don't want him to

find her, but I lie nonetheless. 'I heard her downstairs; she must be getting a glass of water. Go back to bed, you look exhausted.'

Actually, he looks drunk, but he seems happy with my explanation and goes back to their bedroom. When I look past the meadow for a second time my mother has gone.

CHAPTER ELEVEN:

CHAPTER ELEVEN:

THE LADY AND THE LABRADOR

Much to my parents' dismay, after Boxing Day lunch I announce that Izzy, Michael, and I are going Jules' and Eddie's house for a party. Michael looks at his feet as Mother begs us to stay and tries to convince everyone that I am in no fit state to go. Her tone is defeatist though, as she sees the defiance in my eyes. Even Izzy had the sharp end of the tongue earlier when she told me I should not be wearing my wig.

I had held my hand up to silence her, and made her help me cover the scar with an adhesive bandage, muttering crossly, 'As though I would go to a party looking like Frankenstein's *Monster.*'

She eventually gives up and tells Michael to take care of me, and I only feel the slightest trace of guilt that she will be left alone for the afternoon as Father is going to a golf meeting where apparently wives aren't allowed.

'Do you think she'll be OK?' asks Izzy as Michael drives carefully through the snow. 'I don't know why you want to see them anyway today of all days. We could have gone with Mother to see Grandma and Grandad.'

I shrug my shoulders and look out of the window. I suppose I had felt very vulnerable the last time my friends saw me, and I wanted everyone to see I was much better, and one day I would be just like the old me again. I was still fragile, but underneath my wig my scalp was darkening with new hair, and with Izzy's eyebrow magic and my blonde wig, I felt quite pretty. I smoothed down the black velvet of my fitted dress, knowing its figure-hugging style would leave no question in anyone's mind that I was fashionably thin. I wanted to erase the image of Jules' and Eddie's unmasked horror when they saw me in hospital for the first time during chemo and replace it with mild envy at my present fabulousness.

I smile at Michael as he tells me we should take Pinto back to the ranch next week. A look of disappointment must show on my face because he goes on to say that I can ride him every day when I am a little steadier.

I feel very brave and say, 'A child could ride Pinto. I want to ride Blaze,' knowing full well that only Michael had ever ridden the flighty palomino.

'Hmm, we'll see,' he tells me, not looking terribly convinced.

We pull up outside Jules' and Eddie's and the instant we walk through the door I know I have made a terrible mistake. It is only half past three but there are bodies everywhere, and I imagine this house has been the host to anyone not wanting to spend Christmas with their families. I shudder at the memory Jules and I had planned; to start the party on Christmas Eve and try to keep it in full swing until New Year's Eve. It would certainly seem as though all was going to plan so far, and despite her maturity, this was not the place for my little sister.

'Anna!' Jules shrieks, sidestepping the pizza boxes and bottles strewn all over the floor, 'Look, everybody, it's Anna!' She throws her arms around me and I cannot help but smile at my remarkably drunk friend, until she sets her sights upon Michael and my face darkens. 'We haven't met,' she simpers, fluttering her crooked false eyelashes, 'I am Juliet ... Anna's very best friend.' I roll my eyes as she points her ample cleavage in his direction, barely concealed beneath her micro-mini dress. Jules sweeps him away to find drinks and he throws a rather worried-looking glance at me over his shoulder. I sigh disappointedly as I realise everyone is too drunk to notice how well I look, and leave Izzy fending off a boy in a blue rugby kit while I try to find Eddie.

He is collapsed on the sofa, a bottle of his favoured Ouzo in one hand and a burned out cigarette in the other. I nudge him with my foot to no avail. A girl I vaguely recognise offers me some wine, but the smell of weed and stale beer is making me feel sick, not to mention the fact I can barely see a foot in front of me due to smoke.

I find my way to the back door, failing to see Michael and Jules en-route, so I push it open for a little fresh air before I can go back and try again. The cold air hits me like a sheet of ice, but I welcome its freshening reprieve. I take a few deep gulps and think of my mother at home, with her bruised eye and swollen lip. Taking out my phone I dial our landline but she doesn't answer, so I leave a message to say we are not staying and as soon as I find Izzy and Michael we will head back. I presume she has gone to see my grandparents after all, as she had wanted us to this afternoon, and I felt a little cross that I thought this party would be more fun than going to visit them.

I take a few more breaths and am about to head back inside when the most desolate cry I have heard makes me stop and turn back around.

From the height of the little back yard terrace, I can see over the fence to Jules' miserable neighbour's garden, and tied to the washing line is a bereft-looking dog with moulted and matted fur. He is painfully thin and howls a little more loudly before cowering against the yard wall, as a man comes out and promptly kicks his hind quarters. I am about to shout in protest but the sound catches in my throat and I stand absolutely still in shocked silence as the man curls his lip and actually growls at the dog, making it back further away. He raises his hand so the animal flinches, and then staggers back to the house, slamming the door behind him.

I cannot believe what I've just seen, and watch while my heart aches as the dog turns in circles trying to find comfort on the freezing concrete floor. He eventually flops down and another yelp escapes him as his hind leg must have been quite hurt. I look around the yard and see there is no food or water bowl, and he has no shelter from the bitter wind that promised snow through the night.

I take one last look and thank God that the first person I see in the kitchen is Michael. 'Anna, are you OK? You look like you've seen a ghost.' I push past him but grab his hand so I don't lose him again. 'Where's Izzy?'

'She's in the car outside, said she refused to stay a moment longer and to go and fetch you pronto.'

I grab a bottle of brandy from the sideboard and down a couple of glugs as Michael looks at me with a surprised expression.

'Dutch courage,' I tell him. 'Listen to me, this might sound strange but I need you to do something for me.' His handsome face looks dubious and I begin to have second thoughts. I look up at him and remember everything we've been through and consider that perhaps I should be focusing on the two of us and not rescuing neglected animals. I sigh inwardly and tell him, 'Ignore me. It doesn't matter ...' I shake my head and lead him to the front door where Izzy is waiting in the car, looking uncharacteristically cross.

'Don't say it!' I hold my hands up as I slide into the passenger seat while Michael takes the wheel. 'We should have gone to Granny's, I know. Let's just head there now, I think Mother has already gone.'

Izzy does not say anything as Michael pulls out onto the city streets. I wait until we are halfway home, almost approaching the country lanes, before I tell him to turn back around. He stares at me dumbfounded until I breathlessly tell them about the dog, at which point my beloved three-point-turns us back towards the city.

My sister has always been a rescuer of waifs and strays. Of course Mother would never in a thousand years let us keep the poor animal, but if we could just get him home she might let us keep him in the shed for a day or two until Michael can take him to the ranch.

Michael looks at my animated face with amusement. 'You really have this all figured out, don't you, darling?' He sounds cross but a smile plays at his lips. 'And what if my folks don't want another dog about the place?'

I shrug and tell him we would have to find another home for him, but anything would be preferable to leaving him there to freeze or starve to death.

That concludes the discussion, and we focus on hatching a plan to save him. Izzy goes through it a final time before we take the turn onto my old street.

'OK, Michael leave the car in the alley behind his house, then go round front and knock on the door to tell him you're lost and need directions. Keep him talking as long as you can. Anna will get the dog through the backyard gate and I'll keep the engine running while she unties him and fetches him to the car. By that time Michael will have run back around and we're home free!'

She sounds about as convinced as I feel, but not at least attempting to do this just was not an option. We watch poor Michael head round the front and I look behind to see his worried face, clearly not delighted at his task to distract a thug.

Izzy waits anxiously, keeping the engine running as I sigh with relief that the gate is not bolted and opens quietly. I call softly, 'Here, boy,' and the poor soul just looks at me with wary eyes. I wonder what I have gotten myself into, and fear he may bite me as I gently reach behind his collar and begin to untie the tattered rope. I can hear raised voices from inside the house and my hands start to shake uncontrollably, but I have come this far and pull at his now untied collar. Initially refusing to budge, the dog eventually makes a decision to come with me and reluctantly allows me to lead him through the gate, before making it onto the back seat of the car. Izzy burst into to tears when she sees him and I have to hiss to get into the passenger seat.

Michael flies round the corner into view at full sprint and he protests about what a crazy idea that was, and how the man had threatened to punch him, He comes to an abrupt halt when he looks over onto the back seat and at our new companion sat trembling next to me.

By the time we pull into Elm Tree, he's shaking a little less, although he still looks rather bewildered. I can see beneath the grime that he had once been a rather handsome golden Labrador.

To my absolute horror, as we all tumble out of Michael's car, my mother swings open the front door and rests her mortified eyes on our fourth passenger. She is wearing a white Donna Karen suit but as we let the dog out, none of us can quite believe it as she drops to her knees, allowing him to lick her pretty face, oblivious to the muddy paws ruining her designer clothes.

'You poor darling,' she whispers to him, stroking behind his soft ears in a manner that makes his head turn happily upwards. 'Where did you find him?'

'A stray!' I blurt out before she can look at our guilty faces. She might have an unexpected fondness for this dog, but I am certain she would draw the line at theft.

'A stray in this weather, you poor, poor thing.' And with that the raggedy dog follows her obediently into the house while we are left outside stunned.

'But she doesn't like dogs.' Izzy sounds bemused and it was true, we went through the inevitable stage of asking for a puppy throughout our childhood and she had always hidden behind the reasoning that Father would never allow it.

We follow her inside and she is rubbing him gently with an expensive cream bath towel, fresh and warm from the tumble dryer. He seems quite taken with her also, and obediently lifts his paws as she talks to him in a cooing voice.

'His lovely face reminds me of Oscar, your Grandma Beth's little dog.' I shake my head, never remembering her owning a dog.

'We didn't think you liked dogs, Mother.'

She looks up at me sharply, 'It was your father who never wanted animals in the house. He worried they would make too much of a mess,' she adds, but I just manage to hear, 'Take the attention away from him, more like.'

When she is satisfied that the caked mud is mostly gone, three Egyptian cotton bath towels now lie filthy on the kitchen floor. She beckons him to follow her to the fridge and he happily does so as she dices some leftover turkey. 'I know you're hungry, but just a little at a time. We don't want you being sick.'

He nibbles the turkey gently from her fingers and looks so hungry, but my mother is careful and does not feed him too much. She fetches him some water, which he laps at with gusto.

'What about Father?' I say.

'He called earlier and won't be back for two days. These golf gatherings can pan out into other activities.'

With that, we retire into the living room with steaming mugs of hot chocolate while Mother tenderly bathes the cut above the Labrador's eye.

'Do you think we can keep him, Anna?'

'She's very much taken with him but it's inevitable that Father will say no.' I am still in shock at my mother's reaction to the new arrival, and I cuddle into Michael for comfort.

'You did a good thing saving him, Anna. It's unbelievable to me that someone could treat an animal in such a way.'

'We are all children of the same stars.' I tell him, then pause and shake my head having no clue what I meant.

'What?' Izzy asks me, laughing. 'I think we should call him Freedom, because of his great escape.'

I choke on my drink and splutter, 'Freedom? No

way, Izzy! Can you imagine shouting "Freedom" across the park? People will think you're Braveheart.'

On cue, Freedom trots into the living room and Mother settles him in front of the warm fire. 'I think Freedom is a perfect name for him.' She shakes her head sadly. 'Apart from a few little cuts, I think he will be fine. Something tells me he has been much loved before; goodness only knows how he got into that state. Did he have a collar?'

Izzy looks at me guardedly, as I had thrown his collar out of the car window, having no intention of the nasty neighbour ever finding him.

'No collar, Mother. He was a stray, and must have been for months so our conscience is clear and we can find him a good home.'

My mother smiles lovingly at Freedom and I see that if she has anything to do with it, he already has.

***

If you could have taken an image of Elm Tree last Christmas, and compared it to the one of right now, it would have looked remarkably different. Two days have passed since Freedom's arrival and along with his muddy paws, my mother's laughter, and the glorious festive adornments, Elm Tree House is a home full of warmth and happiness.

I look around the kitchen and consider that it

felt more like Grandma's than the bleached and pristine space I was used to. Lillian was so busy fussing over Freedom that she had not been troubled to clear away the toast crumbs, the cutlery, and little jars of honey from breakfast.

I eye the clock nervously, seeing it is almost half past ten and if Father arrives home on time at lunch, he will not only have a heart attack at seeing the new arrival but will be terribly vexed at Mother's abandoned domestic duties.

Feeling very sorry for myself, I begin the arduous task of washing dishes, not at all fair considering I am supposed to be recuperating and had planned to be as bone idle as possible for the foreseeable future. Still, Michael was heading back from the meadow so it would be good for him to see me as a domestic goddess. It may remind him I should make a charming wife.

I smile happily at him, then feel a pull in my heart as he tells me Pinto is in the horsebox and they are ready to go. He sees my face and says, 'I will see you in a couple of hours, Anna. It would be nice if you got to see your father, then Eddie is driving you to mine, I have given him directions ... and considerable gas money!'

I rest my head on his shoulders and he hugs me tightly. 'Don't worry about Freedom. If Malcolm goes crazy just bring him to mine with you. Everything will be fine, darling.'

I look up into his face and tell him I love him,

then morosely wave goodbye as they pull out on to the lane.

As I walk back into the house I take in the dishevelled rooms and paw prints on the wooden floor. I love this new Elm Tree but I know my father will hate it and prefer what I used to call 'The Mausoleum.' I anxiously go to find my mother to see if we cannot tidy up a little, and find her stretched out on the chaise lounge, Freedom draped over her lap.

My eyes widen in horror as I see she is feeding him something from thin crackers, 'Mother, please tell me that is not Father's foie gras?'

She shrugs her shoulders and kisses the top of his golden head. 'Freedom needs fattening up. Your father is quite fat enough.' She laughs like a child as the dog licks her fingers and I worry the world has gone mad.

'Will everyone stop calling him bloody Freedom!' I shout, not meaning to make them both jump. I feel I need to be angry, as I always do when something is out of my control. I look over to the drive and see Eddie pull up, Jules in the front seat beside him. No doubt she wants to see where Michael lives. 'I'm going now so you'll have to see to this mess. I don't envy you having to deal with Father's reaction.'

I leave my mother looking a little lost and she hugs her new friend more tightly.

I grab my bag from the hallway, eager to leave

and follow Michael to Northampton. Eddie had offered to drop me off en-route to his parent's house.

'Damn,' he says, starting the engine. 'No petrol. I'll nip down to village and get some, see you in five.'

'I'll just come with you,' I tell him, annoyed at the delay and wondering why he has no petrol when Michael gave him money.

'No, you won't. I need you to grab me a SatNav. Didn't you say your old man had one?' By the time you've done that I'll be back.'

He says the last part like the Terminator to make me laugh, but I am huffing and puffing, and stomp angrily back to the house.

As I run up the landing I look out of the window and see my mother and Freedom in the meadow. She is throwing him a ball and cheering when he brings it back to her. I cannot help but feel guilty for shouting at her, and think maybe I should apologise before I leave. I've never seen her look so happy; her blonde hair is no longer tied back, and falls prettily around her shoulders as she runs through the long grass. I continue across the landing to my parent's bedroom and become cross once more as it takes me at least ten minutes to find what I am looking for.

I am just about to descend the staircase when I halt suddenly at the top railing. My father is home and yelling at Lillian. I suddenly realise they think they are alone in the house, Izzy is out with her friends and Mother will assume I have already left with Jules. Uncertainly, I take a few steps, then stand back in the shadows as his anger heightens. I peek over the bannister and see my mother protectively holding Freedom's collar, who is not exactly growling at my father but his eyes are wide and his lip is curled back.

'Get that fucking animal out of my house before I skin you alive!'

I'm shocked, as I've never heard him speak so aggressively, and I am frozen into silence, unable to tear my eyes away.

He makes a move towards Freedom and my mother quickly ushers her dog through the door behind her and closes it firmly, her hands trembling.

'Don't you dare!' she yells back at my father. 'Or I swear to God I will kill you!'

My father laughs nastily, and to my horror he grabs her by the throat and pushes her against the wall. Her head makes a sickening thud against the plaster but her eyes do not waver. She stares defiantly at him as he spits in her face with anger.

'I've had enough you, woman! The place is a mess, you have a fucking animal in *my* house, and now you're threatening me? How about I kick you out? Leave your precious house and your daughters to me, Lillian; I'll soon have them straightened out.'

His manner is so vile I cannot recognise him as my father, and I am desperate to cry out but I am stolidly frozen in fear.

'Do it!' she screams, looking manic with resentment. 'But my girls will come with me. We don't need you, Malcolm. I've seen how strong Anna and Isabel are, they aren't like me.'

'You've threatened it for so long but if you ever laid a hand on either of them they would never stand for it. They aren't children!' He releases his grip on her neck and smooths down his jacket.

'You'll never leave, you stupid bitch. Don't chime to me about *your* daughters, they can't stand you. Your miserable face and the tragic martyr you've become. I'm going back to the city, and when I decide to come home I expect that animal gone and this house back to a respectable state.'

My mother holds her throat where he had grabbed it and makes a little laugh. 'You won't come back, Malcolm. I'm filing for divorce and I'll stay at Elm Tree with Izzy and Anna. Should you have anything to say I will tell *everyone* about the monster you are.'

His face has gone deep red and my heart is beating fast, praying he will not attack her again.

'No one will believe you, Lillian.'

'Take that chance.' She turns to face him head on, looking and sounding much braver and to me, quite magnificent. 'Because if they do, and believe me I have collected enough proof over the years, then you will be ruined, Malcolm. No one wants to do business with a cowardly wife beater, and I will drag your name through court like it is mud.'

She opens the door and Freedom no longer looks afraid. In fact, he is barking quite ferociously at my father, who, instead of beating Lillian, picks up his bag and leaves the house in silence.

My mother bends down to praise her dog and looks up in horror as she sees me running down the stairs, tears streaming down my face as I run straight past her, ignoring her desperate voice begging me to come back.

I see my father's Land Rover swerve to miss Eddie's car as he drives down the lane and when I jump in, I tell him there has been a change of plan and demand they take me to the village.

***

After the village, we drive home in silence and I give Jules a less traumatic version of what has happened.

'I knew they weren't happy but I had no idea …' Her voice trails off and I ask them to wait outside as I run back up to the house, finding my mother still pacing the entrance hall. 'Oh Anna.' She reaches for me and I allow her to hold on to me tightly. 'I don't know what to say.' She just looks at me as I hand her the little paper bag I have been carrying.

'I didn't buy any Christmas presents, what with

everything, so I got this for you.'

I don't want to talk yet about what has transpired, and she nods silently, opening the wrapping and tissue paper. Into her hand falls a soft leather collar with a shiny gold disc attached, sparkling as it catches the light and showcasing the engraved golden letters, 'Freedom'.

A tear falls from her eyes as she smiles at me and we beckon him over. The soft collar fits beautifully and we laugh as he barks proudly.

CHAPTER TWELVE:

THE PALOMINO

Izzy and I stay with Mother for a couple of days, which we spend fussing over her, until I can bear his absence no longer and demand to be taken to see Michael so we can spend New Year's Eve together.

I had no idea what to expect, but as we pull up to the ranch I can see it is quite beautiful. All the fences and gates are gleaming white, and although the ground is covered with a thick layer of snow, I can see they will look exquisite against the lush green grass of summer. For acres, I can see horses, and we shout out in delight as a herd of six deer run across one of the paddocks.

'Wow!' Izzy, leans forward as Mother turns the steering wheel. 'This is like Aintree! Your boyfriend must be loaded.'

I frown crossly that she may presume I cared about such things, but was secretly pleased that she looked suitably impressed. I'd had few moments of anxiety regarding Sunrise Ranch, worrying that it may be a little tacky.

As I look along the tree-lined driveway I see an impressive, sprawling manor, built with sandstone and surrounded by well-manicured gardens. To the left of the house is a row of quaint cottages and to the right, the entrance to a grand stable block.

Izzy looks at my worried face and laughs. 'Are we impressed, Madam? Not what you were expecting?'

I tell her to be quiet as Michael comes running out of the house, followed by a Black Labrador and a Jack Russell yapping at his feet. He hugs us all and invites Izzy in for drinks but Mother politely declines and we eye each other nervously. I know she does not want be rude, but I have not told Michael that my father has left, and we certainly do not want to discuss the reasons why.

He raises his eyebrows at me and I smile confidently. 'They have to get back to Freedom, Michael. He has err, separation anxiety!'

He looks unconvinced but welcomes them back anytime, and Mother promises they will as she waves and drives away.

My feeling of shyness returns until Michael pulls me into a bear hug and kisses the top of my head. 'I'm so glad you decided to spend New Year with us, darling. I was disappointed you couldn't come sooner. Is everything all right?'

I reach up on my toes and kiss his smooth jaw. 'It is now,' I tell him, and he picks up my bags and leads me to the house.

His father and step-mother are hovering in the hallway as we ascend the steps and cross the porch. 'Hello. Anna, I'm Michael, M.J.'s father. This is Caroline.' I step forward to shake their hands but they both hug me and I laugh, raising my eyes at Michael when his father calls him M.J.

'Michael Junior,' he tells me, emphasising his American accent and tipping his baseball cap.

'I like it,' I say laughing. 'It's so nice to meet you both. *M.J.* has told me a lot about you, and Sunrise Ranch is beautiful.'

His father smiles warmly and I like him already. He does not look like Michael at all; his eyes and hair are very dark and his skin is deeply tanned. Michael has blue eyes and his hair has grown back dark blond, which he still keeps shaved close to his head.

Caroline looks a little older than my mother, perhaps about forty-five and her brown hair is wild and her curly, her dark eyes sparkling with mischief.

'Well, Anna, we have certainly heard a lot about you over the last few months. We have been positively dying to meet you, but M.J. kept putting us off.'

'Oh, that was my fault, Caroline,' I jump to his

defence. 'I wanted to feel a little better first.'

Caroline puts her arm around me as she leads us into an enormous kitchen, 'He told us how poorly you have you been, and how brave you are.' She sees my slight discomfort and tactfully changes the subject. 'Well, you're here now; that's all that matters, right? I know you're still in recovery but can I tempt you with a little tipple to warm your cockles?'

I nod happily as she pours each of us a warm, heady mixture from a bubbling pan. I smell cinnamon and taste brandy as I drink from the crystal cup and Michael's father tells me it is their special 'hot toddy.'

We talk for a little while and I find myself trying hard to keep my eyes open, but the kitchen is so warm and even the tiniest tot of alcohol goes straight to my head these days.

Michael puts his arm around me and orders me to take a nap before dinner. 'It's only two o' clock, so if you have a few hours sleep now then you might stand a chance of staying awake until midnight with me.'

I let him lead me to a cosy guest room and smile to myself as I slip under the warm blankets. Our surroundings were indeed apt, for wild horses could not have stopped me seeing in the New Year in with Michael.

***

I had ordered him to wake me up no later than seven, but find myself waking up naturally, and the clock on the wall tells me it is only quarter past six. I am pleased to have a little time to freshen up and get changed, and am happier still to find that my room has a pleasant en-suite.

I pick up my wig from beside the bed and head into the bathroom with my overnight bag. I don't think I have time for a shower, and would prefer not to wash away Izzy's carefully sculpted eyebrow magic, so I just wash myself and spray on some floral deodorant and perfume. I look at my reflection critically and pray that Michael does not come in and see me like this. My pretty peach underwear cannot distract from my jutting hips and visible chest bones, and I find myself wishing I could gain even a little weight, but the medication I still need to take has entirely crushed my appetite. I make a mental note to eat more even if I don't really feel like it, otherwise I shall be stuck with this skeletal reflection for the foreseeable future. I shake my head and look more closely at my face as I apply some moisturiser. There are still persistent dark circles under my eyes, but I have grown quite accomplished at hiding those with concealer, and after applying a little blusher, my skin looks glowing. Izzy has shown me how to apply eyebrows but I never get it as perfect as she does, although thankfully now I have a line to follow as some of my brows are slowly returning. I smudge grey kohl pencil around my few lashes and plump up my lips with gloss. When I am satisfied with my face I remove the net that secures my wig and set about replacing the dressing for my scar.

Rather than healing quickly, as Mr Raj had assured it would, the groove of the scar is angry and red, feeling hot to the touch. I sigh inwardly as I hear him telling me sternly not to wear my wig and net for at least six weeks after the operation, but I find I cannot possibly maintain such instruction. I could not have sat opposite Father on Christmas Day with no hair – not that that mattered to me at all any more. I would have rather died than go to Jules' party looking wretched, and I could hardly meet my boyfriend's family looking like I had escaped from a prisoner of war camp.

So the wig had stayed put, and now my scar was swollen and sore. I carefully replaced the dressing and painfully squeezed the net on top of it before gently smoothing down my crowning glory. I know I look so much better, and it would be worth it. I still make a promise to myself that as soon as I get back to Elm Tree I will give my scar a break from the heat and confinement of my fake tresses.

I jump as the door knocks and quickly pull on my robe as Michael enters, carrying a tray. He looks pleased that I am up and I smell freshly ground coffee and warm cookies. 'Did Caroline make those?' I ask, remembering my resolution and biting into one.

'Actually, my father did. He does most of the cooking. Hates English food, the one thing he tries to hold on to is his American cuisine. I think he missed the states more than he tells us. You look beautiful. Have you been awake for long?'

'Just a few minutes or so.' I smile sweetly, despite having just spent forty-five minutes reincarnating myself.

I drink the strong, milky coffee but only manage half a cookie.

'Eat the other half,' Michael tells me in fake annoyance.

'I can't.' I flutter my eyelashes, enjoying his attention to my well-being.

'Eat the other half or I'll be forced to have my wicked way with you.'

I laugh delightedly as I drop the unwanted remains into my coffee cup and Michael delivers on his welcomed threat.

***

Still laughing I dress in my favourite jeans and a light grey cashmere jumper while Michael remakes the bed and dusts cookie crumbs from the covers.

'We'll have dinner soon; it's a family tradition to all have dinner together on New Year's Eve. I'm so glad you're here.' He pulls me closer for a final kiss before we run downstairs, and despite my repressed appetite, my mouth waters at the delicious aromas as we head into the kitchen.

'There you are!' Caroline beckons me over and asks me to open a couple of bottles of wine. There is no time to feel shy or awkward with Caroline and Michael Senior – they have a busy energy that keeps you moving and carries you along with them.

Michael's father sees me struggling with the fancy corkscrew and takes it from me, asking me to fetch some glasses from the cabinet and set them on the table instead. I am happy to do so, and wonder fleetingly why I found it so hard to help my mother lay the table at Elm Tree this Christmas. I pause for a second and remember how flustered she had seemed when she asked me to find the placemats and cutlery and how angrily I had shouted at her, 'Lay the table?! How absolutely charming of you to give your daughter chores when she has just had a tumour removed. *From her brain*,' I had added for good measure, pulling my wig off. Izzy had grabbed the place settings herself and told me to stop shouting and I huffed crossly in front of the fire complaining why dinner was taking so long.

'Are you OK, Anna?' Michael looks at me with worried eyes.

'Yes… I'm fine.' I smile at him and jolt back into action, but not before I recollect how jumpy my mother had been as Father and I critiqued her burned parsnips. I prayed silently that I was not like him.

I have to push these thoughts to the back of my head as a fresh wave of guilt washes over me, and I wonder how I could have been so mean when she was clearly already suffering.

There is no critical judgement at Sunrise Ranch; everyone laughs and talks animatedly while we eat heartily. We had roast turkey and buttermilk biscuits with rich sausage gravy. Some of the food I had never tried before, and it was all quite heavy but I embraced my new resolve to gain weight and ate as much as I could, much to everyone's delight.

Michael Senior particularly approved. 'Jolly good, Anna. You've tried everything. We'll make a smashing cowgirl of you yet!' He says this with a British accent, making us all laugh once more.

I sigh happily and take a little sip of wine as my eyes fall upon a photograph of a young boy with very dark features resembling Michael's father. 'Is that Benji?' I ask, and before my words are spoken I wish I had said nothing, I did not want to be the cause of a downward mood when we were having such a lovely time.

Only Michael's face darkens as Caroline says, 'Yes, Anna. That's Benji. I never got to meet him but we like to talk about him and try to keep his memory alive.' She looks pointedly at Michael, who scrapes back his chair and says he needs some fresh air. I stand up to follow him but his father takes my hand and motions me to sit back down.

'I am so sorry,' I cry. 'I would never want to hurt Michael or upset him. I just saw the picture and he looks so much like you.' I look over to his kind eyes and he tells me not to be upset.

'Michael never got over the death of his little brother. They were very close and he rarely talks about him now, although we wish that he would. What happened was an accident, even I see that now.'

'Did you once blame Michael?'

'No,' he says gently. 'Although I did blame his mother for a while, and I shouldn't have done that. Ben had autism, you see, he lived in a world of his own and we had to watch him very carefully. He was obsessed with water and there was a river flowing through our old ranch in Colorado. It was magnificent and very still on the surface, but strong currents ran underneath.' He pauses for a second and Caroline places her hand over his. 'Renée wasn't watching him, he had run ahead on their walk, and by the time she reached him he had leaned over the bridge to far and fallen in. Renée couldn't swim and the currents carried him down to the shallow pools before Michael could reach him.'

I cry with them and wait only a few moments before I leave them and run to find Michael. He is standing by a railing to the first paddock, stroking a golden horse, his head rested against its neck. I am quite taken away by the horse's beauty; her long mane and tail were shimmering under the moonlight.

'Is this your Palomino?' I ask, feeling the bond between them.

He looks surprised to see me, as though he was lost somewhere in a dream and I had woken him up. 'Yes, come and meet her. This is Blaze.'

I gently hold out my hand and laugh as she breathes warm air over my freezing fingers. 'Hello, Blaze. I used to have hair like yours.' Michael and I both smile at the memory from our days in chemo and he puts his arm around me as I stroke her silky mane. 'Do you think she's warm enough?' I ask him, although as I slip my fingers under the blanket around her I feel she is quite warm underneath. Michael just holds me tighter.

'I was two when Benji was born. I can't really remember much of him being a baby but when he started to walk, boy, did he follow me everywhere!' Michael wipes a tear from his eye, and my heart breaks for him as I listen silently. 'We knew he was different when he was really young, he didn't like to be touched or cuddled too tightly and used to hate wearing clothes until one of my Aunties bought him Aquaman pyjamas for his fourth birthday. Then they were pretty much all he wanted to wear. I used to read him comic books about a superhero that lived underwater and could talk to sea creatures telepathically.' He laughed, 'When I say read, I mostly used to point at the pictures and make the stories up. Benji really loved them, but then he became obsessed with the river, believing he could dive and swim like Aquaman, so we had to faze him out.'

'Faze him out?'

'Yes, we had to gradually introduce new comics and characters but it took a long time to curb the obsession. I think Benji knew what we were doing so he went deeper inside himself; he never lost his fixation with deep water, although eventually he stopped making a fuss when we fenced off the river and never let him walk the ranch alone. He never talked much to begin with, but began to live in near silence as he grew older. The only things he couldn't resist were trains and tractors, so we indulged him and communicated through the things he liked.'

Michael is quiet for a few moments so I ask him tentatively, 'Were you there when he fell into the water?'

'I was riding on the ranch. It was three days before my tenth birthday so Benji would have been seven. My mom had taken a lame horse for a lead walk along the trail path to see if she was better and had taken Ben with her for some fresh air. I could see them from where I was riding a little further up the hill, and he stayed just a stone's throw in front of her, looking up at the sky and then stopping to touch the ground. It was a funny habit of his. She only looked away for a couple of seconds. The mare was showing signs of discomfort and my mother bent down to check her front hoof. When she looked back up he was gone and she knew instinctively he had run to the little wooden bridge. I knew in a heartbeat as she screamed his name that he was already there, but I galloped towards them and dived into the river where the currents wane a little.'

I know Michael is crying, and let him take comfort against Blaze's solid neck as I have no idea how to console him.

'He was already lying there, floating on the surface with his face down in the water. When he had jumped or fallen from the bridge the currents would have pulled him under. I knew these waters like no-one else, I knew where they looked calm and inviting but were ferocious underneath. I pulled him out and breathed in to his mouth the way my father had taught me, but his head was bleeding and I could tell he was gone. My mom just screamed and screamed, "Save him, Michael!" and I couldn't.'

'Michael, you were ten, no one could have expected you to save him.' I pull him towards me despite his protests and stroke his back, now wracked with sobs. He tries to compose himself and tightens a loose buckle on the horse's blanket.

'My father found us like that, and went off at my mom for not watching him. I left them screaming at each other, thinking how Benji would have hated that. He liked quiet. She left the next day, and I haven't seen her since.'

'Michael. I am so sorry.'

'It's OK. This is why I don't talk about it. It's just too painful for me; he was too young to die and should still be here with us.'

I truly hate myself for thinking that if his brother had not died, Michael would never have moved to England and I could have still been lost in a nightmare.

'You saved me, though,' is all I can tell him, and he presses his cold lips against mine for a moment.

***

After only a few hours sleep, we wake up before dawn on New Year's Day, sleepy-eyed and feeling that we are closer than ever. He looks at my scar with concern and suggests I go to see Mr Raj.

'Are you crazy?' I shout, louder than I intend and hastily soften my voice. 'What I mean is, I don't want to go back until I absolutely have to.'

'Which is when?'

'Two weeks' time, I think. What are we doing today?' I am anxious to change the subject.

'I have a surprise for you. Get dressed. Something warm!' He winks as he rushes downstairs and I know he is taking me riding. I am under strict instructions from my mother not to ride while I am here, and it is with a little guilt that I pull on my jeans and run to the bathroom to get ready.

Michael is waiting by the stables, but instead of seeing two horses, he stands only with Blaze, who is unsaddled and wearing a simple bridle.

I look at him disappointedly as he leads her to the mounting block and climbs up.

'I'm not coming with you?' I ask, and he smiles and shuffles backwards, tapping the little space in front of him. I laugh delightedly and am up in front of him in seconds, smiling as he places a firm arm around my waist and the other holds the reins. I feel a little unsteady without a comfortable saddle beneath me, and he tells me to hold on to her mane.

We ride around the breath-taking grounds, magnificently highlighted by the orangey glow of the sunrise. We walk steadily along little trails, through silent woods and a shallow ford, and I cry out in delight to see a fox and a deer.

'This is the best day of my life,' I tell him and turn my head back to find his lips for a kiss. He pulls Blaze to a halt at the neck of the woods, which showcases the exploding sunrise and makes the white snow glisten like a fairy tale.

'Did you like your Christmas present, Anna?'

'Yes, of course.' I stumble over the words and do not know why I'm nervous. 'I've almost read all of it. I know the difference between Piebald and Skewbald; I know that an Appaloosa has unusual dappled markings over their hind-quarters ...'

My voice trails away as reaches around me and places a little box in my right hand.

'What is this?' I ask him unsteadily.

'That is your real Christmas present. Open it.'

I slip off my gloves and open the little gold clasp to reveal a beautiful diamond ring, gleaming in the early morning sun light.

'Marry me, Anna.'

I pause for half a second before Blaze throws her head up and I shout out 'Yes!' and spin from my waist to throw my arms around him.

CHAPTER THIRTEEN:

BACK TO BLACK

As we pull up outside Elm Tree a week later, I am thrilled to see Izzy, Freedom, and Mother shivering on the front step to greet us. They knew we were engaged, I had called as soon as we had stabled Blaze and run back to the ranch. It only disgruntled me a little to discover that Mother had already known as Michael had asked her permission when he could not make contact with my father. He was definitely suspicious that he had left again so suddenly, but seeing my expression had not pressed me for further information.

'Congratulations to both of you!' she cries and as we hurry towards them, we all hug and I hold on to my mother for a moment longer, as apart from eating more, one of my New Year's Resolutions was to be a better daughter. There has been none of the expected exclamations that we were too young to be contemplating marriage and I loved her for that. My illness had taught me that time comes with no guarantee, and that I needed to live for now. She kisses the top of my head and ushers us into the house, which to my delight is decorated with banners and seemingly any other 'Congratulations on your Engagement!' paraphernalia they could find.

I hug Izzy again and tell her she would have to help me plan the wedding, which we want to take place the following New Year. 'I don't want too many people, though,' I say anxiously, shuddering at the thought of Jules and Eddie turning up drunk with all the rest of my old acquaintances. 'But Izzy, you will be my bridesmaid, won't you?'

'Of course I will.' She looks at me fondly then we both turn to look at our mother, sensing apprehension as we all consider how Father might fit into all this. Not at all, if I have my way.

I take Michael's hand and we sit by the fire. Mother brings cups of tea as we fuss over Freedom, who is looking decidedly different to the dog we rescued a few weeks ago. He has already gained a little weight, and has been lovingly groomed so his coat is shining. Even Lillian looks better; her air of sadness is gone and she has rosy cheeks from the long strolls they have taken together. I was thankful to hear her occasionally shorten his name to Fred or Freddie, and I latch on to this, feeling slightly relieved I may be saved from shouting 'Freedom' across the busy village common.

'He is so well trained,' Mother tells us proudly. 'He runs straight back to me the second I call him, and he stops and sits next to busy roads.' She rubs his ears affectionately. 'You're a little genius aren't you, Fred?'

I interrupt her loudly, feeling he had had enough attention for now, and tell them to look at my engagement ring.

I am once again a little put out as Mother tells me Michael had already shown it to her when he asked for her blessing, but I do try to remember my three-day-old resolution and just smile sweetly as she goes on to tell me how stunning it is.

'Where would like to get married?' Izzy probably hopes it will be somewhere exotic.

'In the village church, maybe.' I look shyly at Michael. 'Then perhaps a small gathering here or at the ranch, depending on where we are.'

My mother has a worried look on her face so I try to reassure her. 'Michael's parents are going travelling in January next year. They've always wanted to, but needed to wait until Michael was completely recovered before they could leave him to manage Sunrise.'

'I'll be one hundred per cent this time next year,' Michael continues as Mother looks progressively anxious, 'so that will free them to live out their lifelong dream abroad without worrying about leaving me alone. They have asked Anna and I if we will take over the ranch after we're married. Of course she'll finish her A Levels first and I will show her the ropes, but she can travel between there and Elm Tree until it's all settled. Lillian, it really is not that far – only forty-five minutes if the traffic's good – and we shall expect to see you and Freedom every weekend!'

I try to conceal my look of horror as Izzy giggles and Mother looks delighted.

I climb up the stairs to my room, leaving them talking while I take a few moments to myself. As promised, I take off my wig and place it back on the stand Mother bought for me. Leaning forward in my dressing room mirror I see that the scar is still swollen and painful. I curse inwardly that it should have been enough to have a bloody brain tumour without this on top of everything. I remember Mr Raj prescribing me some healing cream, which I had not used as he told me it was only if the scar did not heal by itself. I rummage around in the drawers to find it as Izzy walks in.

'What you lost?' she asks me, plonking herself down on the bed.

'My scar isn't healing. Mr Raj gave me some cream and I can't find it.'

Izzy backs out the room and returns a few moments later with the little tube. 'We may have borrowed it for Freedom,' she tells me. 'Mother was scared to take him to a vet about the cut above his eye in case someone had reported him missing. She called a vet instead and they said that cream was suitable as it is mildly antibacterial.'

Should I have had to listen to her nervous ramblings a month ago about how our mother had stolen her daughter's scar cream for a bloody dog, I could not have been held responsible for my actions. Now I sigh deeply and ask her, 'Did it work?'

'Oh yes!' She sounds terribly relieved. 'He healed up in no time, bless him.' Her voice trails off as she sees my expression and she offers to help me.

'You have to clean it with those sterile wipes first,' she twitters on. 'The vet told us to use those as well.'

I frown crossly but say nothing as she puts on gloves and gently cleanses my scalp. I am reminded of Dr. Braby on the ward and suddenly feel incredibly tired. I absently listen to Izzy telling me off for wearing my wig and suddenly meet her eyes in the mirror.

'I never thanked you.'

'What for?' she asks, looking confused.

'The way you were when I was in hospital, it really got me through everything. Knowing that I had you ... and Mother,' I add, smiling.

'We love you, Anna. It's been hell for us too;

worrying you might not get better. Honestly, if it hadn't been for Michael, we would never have got through this. You have changed so much since you met him, you seem ... happy.'

'Despite everything?' I say pointing to my bereft hair and ugly scar.

'Despite everything,' she says, and gives me a hug.

***

Michael stays for as long as he can before heading home to help his parents. They had a party of twelve booked in for the fifteenth of January, so he had to return to contribute with the preparations.

I mope around for a few days, but secretly I am exhausted trying to look good for him all the time. It is quite blissful not to bother with makeup for a little while and I am less self-conscious about not wearing my wig. Izzy is back to school so I spend my days mostly between Mother and long phone conversations with Michael.

'How are you feeling today?' he asks, as he always does.

'I'm fine.' I tell him, although for the last week or so this has not been entirely true. I'm still finding it difficult to eat despite having had my medicine doses reduced, and although I haven't seen him since I was discharged, Mr Raj had told me my symptoms should gradually disappear. But I felt dizzy, my headaches have returned, and I am permanently tired. I had almost fallen last week when I had run up the stairs hearing my mobile ringing from my room, and had had to grab on to the bannister at the top, suddenly feeling I may pass out.

This had happened a lot before my diagnosis, but I had been drinking and partying so much, I thought feeling dizzy was normal.

'Anna, are you still there?' Michael's voice breaks through my reverie.

'Yes, I'm here. Are you still coming to my appointment next week?'

'Of course I am, angel. January twenty-second, three-thirty.' I smile at his American accent, which is prominent at more times than others, especially when he recites dates and times. I hear my mother calling for me so I roll my eyes and tell him I have to go.

'What is the emergency?' I ask her as I find them in the kitchen, Freedom her constant companion. I pat his head while she tells me dinner is ready, and I recoil as she lifts the pan lid and a wave of nausea hits me. I feel very hot at the back of my head and my mother tells me, 'That is enough, Anna. You've looked wretched and wan for almost a week. I haven't said anything thus far, but we need to bring your appointment with Mr Raj forward. I'm sorry, darling, but you should be feeling better and something isn't right.'

I sit at the breakfast bar and place my burning

temples against the cool work surface. 'It's back, isn't it?' I ask without looking up. 'They said it might come back and it's back. Like the fucking Terminator.'

***

Mr Raj agreed to see me earlier and booked a new appointment for the seventeenth. I sit nervously outside his room but this time I am not alone. Izzy and my mother are to the left of me, bickering about Izzy biting her nails. Michael is on my right, holding my hand, and Freedom is waiting in the car with a blanket. Mr Raj smiles as he sees us and pulls up a few extra chairs. I determinedly avoid the Alice in Wonderland chair he gestures me towards and he nods understandingly as I plonk myself on an uncomfortable plastic seat. It reminds me of the chairs from school and I suddenly think of an assistant whose chair we once pulled out from under her.

'So, Anna.' I try to read the consultant's face but he stays neutral as always. 'Thank you for undergoing more tests for me earlier. I trust they weren't too unbearable?' I hope to God he is not remembering my peek-a-boo bra.

'They were fine,' I mutter, hardly remembering the physical exam another doctor in neurology had carried out that morning. A nurse had taken blood and urine samples and I had been waiting for three hours for him to take off his glasses and tell me

230

once again that I have cancer.

'I have your results here …' He begins slowly, but I cannot take any more.

'I'll save you the bother, Mr Raj, as this cannot be a part of your *job* you are particularly fond of.' I say 'job' in a derisory manner just to be sure he knew how much I thought his chosen vocation sucked. 'My brain tumour has returned with a vengeance, this time it is not possible to operate and instead of kindly allowing me to die with an ounce of dignity the first time round you have successfully prolonged my suffering and pain a further four months.'

I smile with satisfaction as Mr Raj does remove his glasses as predicted.

'No, Miss Winters. Your cancer has not returned.' He smiles in a friendly manner that I happen to find quite smug. 'You're pregnant.'

That wipes the smirk off my face.

***

I have never *ever* thought about having children. To me that is something for thirty-year-olds when they have exhausted every excuse not to. I look around at the stunned faces. Michael looks shocked but delighted; Mr Raj still looks a little smug like he has got one over on me, and Izzy and my mother look like they can barely contain themselves. I can tell they are beyond relieved that my cancer has not returned. Mother looks very anxious but somehow happy at the same time. As I watch them looking back at me expectantly, I wonder why it is that I do not feel the same. I sense a foreboding dark cloud returning.

CHAPTER FOURTEEN:

LITTLE SEED

We spend the next hour with The Mad Hatter as he tells me I would appear to be around three weeks pregnant, which to me means I became pregnant on Boxing Day.

Michael cannot stop smiling and my mother and Izzy keep telling me I am delighted into shock. Mr Raj looks at me dubiously and goes on to tell me that it is usually better to wait between six months to a number of years before conceiving a child after cancer treatment.

My spirits lift as I hold on to the possibility he is telling me I should not continue with the pregnancy.

'What do you mean? Is it dangerous to get pregnant after chemo?'

'Well, Miss Winters we will need to refer you to an obstetrician, but eggs damaged by chemotherapy are thought not to have left the body until six months *after* treatment cessation.'

Michael looks worried as I continue my enthusiastic line of interrogation. 'So my eggs are still damaged, right? This baby could end up looking like a Chernobyl trout with three heads and webbed feet?'

'Anna, no! My goodness, you do get carried away with yourself at times!' Mr Raj gives a rare laugh and turns to Michael, hoping for a more reasonable response.

'Your baby stands every chance to be happy and healthy, but seeing as you have both been ill I think it should be wise to refer you immediately for a check-up. I shall confer with your obstetrician regarding past and present medications. In the meantime, Anna, I am pleased to see you have gained a little weight.'

Despite the bombshell he has happily dropped on my wrought nerves, I am surprised that he has taken this opportunity to insult me. I pull myself up and suck my tummy in a little.

'Do you think I'm fat now, *doctor*? How very kind of you. Wait till you see me in nine months' time, then you can really have a pop at me.'

I leave them to arrange my next appointment as I storm out of the stifling office and along to the car ahead of them.

As I hasten down each corridor I feel more and more doomed. The mutant embryo inside me will grow bigger every day, and instead of never stepping a foot inside a hospital again, which I had been so determined to do, I would now be expected to attend further testing, ante-natal classes, and God only knows what else.

I didn't have time to consider that I had been convinced my cancer was returning, and that perhaps this should have been a welcome reprieve from the thunderous black cloud. I step outside and find a bench outside the main entrance, taking in great gulps of air. A man is standing next to me in blue pyjamas, trying to smoke a cigarette while manoeuvring around his drip stand.

'Can I have one, please?' He turns to face me and I have to stop myself from recoiling in horror as I see that his skin is quite yellow and he has a Frankenstein scar of his own zigzagging across his throat. He eyes my own jagged wound and nods approvingly, handing me a cigarette and lighting it for me.

We smoke in companionable silence, two rebels disregarding Doctor's orders: Frankenstein's monster and his bride.

I feel a moment of grim calmness until I hear Lillian's piercing screech as she sees the offending Silk Cut.

'Anna!' she hisses at me, swiping it from between my fingers then throwing it to her left as though it were an undisposed bomb. 'What are doing, you stupid girl? You're carrying a baby; if you smoke so do they!'

She looks so horrified that even my partner in crime gives me a disapproving look before shuffling away from the drama.

I'm about to shout something at her until she asks me, 'What if Michael saw you? He is so happy, Anna. This is not just about you, please try to remember that.'

I open my mouth but then close it abruptly as I see his Jeep pulling into the lay-by, Izzy's concerned face peering from the window beside him. I have just enough time to whisper angrily at my mother, 'If it's not just about me, Mother, then why do I have to carry the damn thing?'

Despite me asking everyone to say nothing of my current state, over the first trimester of pregnancy I receive visits from two very excited parties. The first little excursion to the freak show is partaken by Michael's parents, and the second by my overjoyed grandparents.

'I'm sorry, darling.' Michael laughs at my cross face a few weeks later as Caroline and his father pull up outside Elm Tree. 'They knew something was going on and I had to tell them!' He leaves me to get changed as I sigh despondently.

I am beyond tired. My breasts are swollen and sore and I have mood swings Joan Collins would be proud of. New Year resolutions forgotten, I almost murdered my mother when she bought a baby book 'to help to prepare me.' They were all squashed together cooing over pictures, and unable to suppress my curiosity I walked casually past the chaise longue and peeked over their shoulders. The picture of a baby at eight weeks nearly floored me and my worst fears were confirmed that he or she would be an alien. My only ray of light at this point was that I could defer the rest of my A Level studies for at least another year. A nagging part of me ached for the days when those exams were all I had to worry about. When had I been so discontent?

I shake my head at the thought, reminding myself that had I not fallen ill, I would not have met Michael. This was his baby, and he was so happy I desperately tried to go along with their charade as best I could.

I resisted the urge to cause another scene and crept hastily back up to my room. I had already attended a health check with a specialist in maternal-foetal medicine, and had stubbornly refused to look at the screen after she pointed out his features and all I could see was a Space Invader. Michael's eyes had never left the screen and when he finally met my eyes, he mistook my tears for ones of joy.

I was barely pretending to be in any way enthusiastic about a single aspect of my pregnancy, but they were all treating me with gloves and putting my depression down to 'hormones.' I called one expression they were all equally fond of the 'hormone eye roll', which came into play after one of my frequent outbursts.

I look at Michael's family and feel utterly distraught that I need to confront them so miserably. I even decide not to wear my wig hoping it will wipe the smiles off their faces as I slowly descend the stairs.

It does not.

***

Michael tries to hold me in bed one night and I resist the urge to shrug him off me. 'Anna, tell me what is wrong. How can you be so unhappy when we are going to be so blessed? Are you really just scared or is there something you should tell me?'

I know that this is my chance to open up to him completely, as he has avoided this conversation at all costs so far. I want to tell him that I am not scared, I am terrified beyond recognition. The last time something was growing uninvited inside me it nearly killed me, and I had spent the worst days of my life inside that hospital. For almost twelve weeks I have had to return every fortnight, each time hating myself for hoping that during a scan my baby's heartbeat would not echo around through the room as it always did. I want to tell Michael how my heart had lifted during my first appointment as a doctor had told me to be prepared that the pregnancy might not survive full term. That our illnesses and treatment may have prevented a healthy conception and a hospitable environment in which it may grow. She may have thought my eyes had widened in dismay rather than optimism.

'Anna, did you hear me?'

Of course I can't speak such atrocities, to a man who has brought me so much happiness and unconditional love. I close my eyes and pretend to sleep as he moves away from me.

I am sixteen weeks pregnant and the little seed determinedly and stubbornly grows within me.

Chapter Fifteen:

REMEMBER ME

I am reaching the end of my third trimester and everyone tells me I am blossoming. It is the eleventh of September and the baby is due in two weeks.

I have tried to mask my worries and fears, and although Michael does not press me, we both feel an ever extending gulf between us. I never thought I would feel so separate from this man I loved so dearly and I could not help but blame the entity growing inside me.

I cannot bear to look at my body as I feel ridiculous, and when I was in a particularly self-deprecating mood one morning, I stripped down to my underwear to critique more closely the damage caused by pregnancy.

My arms and legs were still thin, but every finger and each ankle were puffed and swollen. I had breasts beyond recognition, filled to bursting with milk in a manner that repelled me, with dark brown, saucer-like circles around each nipple. From my protruding belly button to my groin, a dark-shaded line had formed and I looked as though I had swallowed a space hopper. The baby moved and kicked inside me, making me breathless and uncomfortable, and for the best part of nine months I felt I had had no energy at all.

Izzy walks into the room to find me sitting at the base of the bed in my dressing grown, crying into my hands.

'Anna, what's wrong?' she asks me in exasperation, and I have no doubt she will have executed the hormone eye roll.

'I just looked in a mirror.' I spat at her, glad to have someone as an outlet for my rage.

'But you're beautiful! Your hair is growing back thick and fast, your skin is glowing, and you are still very slim. Once the baby is born you will have your figure back in no time.'

'Beautiful?!' I muster up as much contempt as I can. 'I'm a fat mess, Izzy. I can hardly walk for the pain in my back; I just waddle around this house all day while you whisper behind my back. Don't think I haven't noticed.'

'We're all worried about you, Anna. We know how unprepared you were for this but even Mr Raj says you are thriving and pregnancy has suited you. I just wish you could be a little more pleased about this new baby, and stop worrying he won't be OK. Just because you've been ill doesn't mean it will affect you giving birth to a healthy child, and all the scans have confirmed this.' She rubs my hand reassuringly but I swipe it away.

'The baby? I'm not worried about the baby, Isabel! I'm worried about what it has done to my body, and why that during a time in my life I should have been recovering from cancer it is subjecting me to a further nine months of torture! I can't sleep, I have a body like a beached whale, I am aching all over and have never felt less attractive in my life. Milk is seeping out of my nipples, I'm constantly needing to pee ... Do you know Michael hasn't been near me for weeks?'

I fail to mention that the last time Michael tried to make love to me I had kicked him in the shin.

'Nobody asked *me* if I wanted this baby, I don't even like children, and I have no clue how to be a mother. All I wanted was to recover from my illness and plan the wedding of my dreams, and now I don't even have the energy to do that. We won't be getting married at New Year, all I will be doing is changing nappies and getting puked on. This baby has ruined everything.' I know I should stop but I can't end my rant. All of my fear and anxiety is pouring out of me like an uninterrupted waterfall.

'What chance does it stand? *Both* parents have had cancer and let's face it, we don't exactly have a promising gene pool. My father is a wife-beater, my mother is a bag of nerves, Michael's brother was two cents short of a shilling, and his mother a neglectful abandoner! I should have had an abortion then everything would have stayed the same.'

I have shocked my sister into silence but we both look up, horrified to see Michael standing in the doorway. He turns on his heel, looking so hurt I feel I have been punched in the stomach.

I try to stand to go after him but Izzy pulls me back without difficulty, 'Let him go, Anna. Give him a few moments.'

I am crying steadily and she puts her arm around me, holding me close.

'I know this has been too much for you, but none of us ever considered you would choose not to continue with pregnancy. We saw it as such a blessing. I'm sorry for not listening to you but maybe a small part of you really does want this? You *never* do anything you don't want to, so perhaps this is the right thing for you and you just can't see it yet?'

I look up into her naïve face, certain that she is wrong, but I have caused enough anguish for one day.

'Maybe,' I tell her, and rise awkwardly to my feet to find Michael.

***

I find him in the meadow throwing a stick for Freedom, and his body visibly tenses as I breathlessly approach them.

'Are you OK?' he asks me as I breathe heavily, perhaps a little heavier than necessary as he may be less cross with me that way.

'Michael, I am so sorry for what I said – About Benji and the baby. I don't really want a termination; I am just so bloody tired I cannot think straight.'

He looks at me steadily and I know he does not accept my lie about not wanting to end the pregnancy.

'I hardly know you these days, Anna. You won't talk to me about anything. We're supposed to be getting married and I feel like sometimes I have no idea what is going on inside your head. All of this has happened so quickly but I thought it would be our way of sticking our fingers up to cancer, turning something negative into good. Most people never have the opportunity to realise how precious life is until they face losing it. Every day now is a blessing and I presumed you felt the same.'

I shrug my shoulders and refrain from mentioning that perhaps if he had been the one waddling around like a disabled duck for three months he might not be feeling quite so blessed.

'When Mr Raj told me you were pregnant I felt like the luckiest man in the world. I thought he was going to say you were ill again, that I might lose this veracious, beautiful girl I had planned to spend the rest of my life with.' He shakes his head sadly. 'It was beyond imagining that instead of losing life, we had created a new one together.'

I look up at Michael and hate myself once more, wishing I could see the world the way that he does.

'I'm scared I'll mess it up!' I try to sound vulnerable so he will comfort me as he does so adeptly when I am afraid. 'What if I'm like my father? What if I turn out to be cruel and heartless like he was?'

I surprise myself as I say these words for I had kept this fear buried for as long as possible, but Michael does not cajole me as I imagined he would and grabs my shoulders so I am forced to face him.

'Then don't let that happen, Anna,' he tells me unlovingly. 'For once in your life take some responsibility for the way you are and stop blaming cancer or your upbringing. Be present in your own life and make a decision to be the best parent to this child that you can be, without question or compromise. This is no time to be selfish and self-indulgent. Those days have gone and in less than two weeks your only concern will be our baby. If you cannot put our child's needs before your own then I will raise the baby without you. I love you, Anna, but you are pushing me too far. Please stop making this about you. I've been thinking about this a lot, Anna, and I'm going up to the ranch for a few days. I think we need some space.'

I'm not entirely sure whether or not this is the right time to tell him that I think my waters have just broken.

* * *

The next few hours of my life could only be described as complete pandemonium. Michael had been frozen to the spot since I told him my waters had broken, muttering that it was too soon, but I was certain that the moment I had been dreading for the best part of nine months had arrived. I shouted for my mother, who came running out to see me holding my dressing gown against my groin and knew in an instant we were ready to launch. She untied her apron, shouted something to Izzy about my bags, and jolted Michael into sudden action by telling him to bring the Jeep round. I looked to her with desperation as she ran over and helped me into the house, bolting the kitchen door behind us. Freedom looked concerned and to my annoyance, she took the time to bend down and stroke his ears softly, telling him to be a good boy and that we would not be long.

I didn't have time to be angry with her because the dull ache in my womb that had been present all day suddenly intensified, making me cry out in pain. 'Oh God, you're having contractions,' said Izzy breathlessly, a mixture of excitement and high anxiety in her voice.

I took a moment to shoot her an evil look, annoyed that she knew I was having a contraction before I had even realised what they were. I should not have been surprised, seeing that she had read every single one of the baby books I had tossed aside, and had already bought herself a 'World's Best Aunty' T-shirt. She would not have dared tell me, but I had found the offending garment in her drawer when searching for a jumper.

Izzy ignored me, and set a stop clock on her phone as we headed to the front of the house where Michael was waiting. I clambered onto the Jeep's back seat, still in my white linen dressing gown soiled with a pinkish-tinged fluid. My mother and Izzy jumped in either side of me, Lillian already on her mobile to the maternity ward to tell them we were on our way.

I doubled over for a second time, my face twisted in pain, and cried out as another contraction grasped my abdomen with a forceful blow.

'Four minutes!' shouted Izzy and I squeezed her hand as hard as I possibly could until she yelled in anguish herself.

Michael turned to face me for a second and our eyes met. He recognised my expression of pure fear and gave me a look of pure love. 'You will be all right, my darling. I'm not going anywhere; we will get through this together.'

I read between the lines and took a moment's comfort knowing I was perhaps his darling once more.

**

A small team of medical staff are waiting for me at the ward entrance and I am in too much pain to argue as they whisk me away in a wheelchair. I am changed swiftly into a gown as they let Michael and my mother into the room, who stand by my head as a device is tied around my stomach to measure the baby's heartbeat. Another unbearable cramp takes hold of me, and does not seem to release for a lifetime. When I open my eyes the nurses look concerned as they study a small monitor. One of them reaches across me and hits a red button.

I am doubled over in pain once more and tell them I need to push, but a midwife I do not recognise is huddled with the other nurses around the monitor. I scream for pain relief but no one listens as I hear Izzy telling the doctor that I last ate less than two hours ago.

Finally, the midwife acknowledges my presence and comes over to the bed while a nurse with a bag of fluids begins to attach an intravenous line to my arm. I am too alarmed to protest and hold more tightly to Michael's hand as the midwife tells me that my baby's heart rate is dropping quickly.

Another member of staff is rubbing a cool gel

over my stomach and I recognise her from my last ultrasound.

'Try not to worry, Anna. I'm going to take a look at what's happening.' She efficiently carries out her task and the midwife returns to my side a short time later to tell me that the umbilical cord is in front of the baby's face. With every contraction my stomach is cutting off its air supply.

'Will I die?'

He looks confused at my question but hastens to tell me that I need to have an emergency C-section and orders the nurses to prepare me for theatre.

I must not be making sense because Michael is the one everyone addresses as I am whisked away in the confusion to be given an epidural. I am asked to lean forward and an incredibly painful injection is administered to my back before I am wheeled into an operating room. My legs begin to feel numb and I panic, asking one of the staff where Michael was.

She turns as though she is surprised to hear from me and smiles reassuringly. 'He's on his way. Just getting him prepped for theatre.'

I wondered fleetingly if Michael was having an operation also. I have heard people using the expression that their teeth were 'chattering with fear' and this is happening to me now as I realise I can no longer feel my legs. The midwife enters the room with Michael, both dressed in green gowns and masks, and I only recognise my fiancé as he is always the tallest person in any room.

I hold on to his blue eyes and he tells me not to be afraid, that I will not feel any more pain and my legs are supposed to be numb.

'But I can feel *something*!' I tell him desperately, as the midwife hovers by my legs. 'What if I feel them cut into me? Michael help me, I can't do this. I can't!'

He looks afraid as he bends forward to kiss my clammy brow and strokes the feathery hairs from my forehead.

'Can you feel this, Anna?'

'Feel what? I can't feel anything!' My voice rises in panic but the surgeon soothingly tells me he was pinching my legs and the epidural has worked. 'We need to deliver your baby, so please try to relax.'

He nods to Michael and as my teeth chatter, he talks to me about how everything is going to be fine, and in a few minutes our baby will be born. We still don't know the sex of the baby as I had refused the option. I'm not sure why I did, as Michael had wanted to know, but I had grasped every opportunity for control over the last few months, of which there were not many.

I feel uncomfortable pulling and digging in my abdomen but I was happy that the excruciating pain of labour had released its determined grasp over me.

I look up at Michael's pale face and his eyes

widen as the surgeon lifts our baby from my body.

'A girl,' he announces, but my heart stops at his concerned tone. My daughter is bundled into a blanket and for the most fleeting moment, held in front of me, before they leave me paralysed and helpless as she is whisked away through the screen doors.

I had no moment to feel anything when I saw her for the first time. She was a strange colour and her eyes had been closed. If she had only opened them for a second to look at me, I may have connected to her, but she was gone from me and Michael can offer me no words of comfort.

***

It feels like hours later that I am waking up in recovery. I do not remember falling apart but Michael tells me that I became very distressed when they took her away, and administered morphine while I was being stitched.

'You fell asleep,' he tells me, looking at me with love, reassured that my distress was a good sign that I cared deeply for our little girl.

I've no idea how I feel as he tells me that she needed oxygen, which she was responding well to in the special baby unit.

'Can I see her?' I ask him.

'Not yet, darling. Not yet.'

By the time they deem it suitable to let a mother see her own child, I am becoming increasingly cross. Only one person at a time stays with me while the others troop off to see the baby as she regains her strength. I do not feel that enough emphasis and concern have been bestowed upon me, considering the horrific ordeal I have recently endured.

My mother mistakes my disgruntlement for anxiety.

'Don't worry, they will bring her soon. In a little while when the epidural has worn off they may let us take you to see her.'

I look at my mother as though she has gone mad. 'I will not be sitting in that contraption again, ever. *They* can bring *her* to me.'

Over the next few hours I complain incessantly of the pain I am suffering, so by the time they finally bring the baby to see me, I am quite doped up.

'Here she is, darling.' Michael lifts her tenderly from the little trolley as a nurse fusses about him. He looks confident and delighted as my mother props a pillow behind me and he places the sleeping baby in my arms. I feel such a surreal feeling of detachment from the entire affair that I wish for a moment they were not all watching me so intently. Under their scrutinising gaze I hold my breath as I look at her and consider that she looks much more appealing now than she did a few hours ago. Her hair is smooth and of the palest blonde, she has a tiny little nose and rosebud lips, which she smacks together a couple of times as I hold her awkwardly in my arms. As she opens her eyes for a flutter we look at each other for the very first time. I look over at Michael, who is smiling at me with expectation so I smile back at him.

I take another peek at my daughter before my head starts swimming and someone takes her from me. As I look at her beautiful little face, I feel nothing.

***

In less than a week we are all inevitably ensconced back at Elm Tree. My old room has been made into a recovery room for mother and baby. I am thankful for my caesarean section now, because despite the pain, it has posed me the advantage of requiring a great deal of help with the baby. I can't pick her up, and only have to endure moments here and there when Izzy or Michael would pass her to me as I lie in bed. A concerned midwife eventually gave up on demonstrating breastfeeding techniques, telling me I needed to relax, so I was happily now expressing my milk, meaning less contact still. Mother was truly concerned, but I managed to persuade her to give me a little more time to get used to everything and I would smile sweetly to reassure her.

The moment they all left I would cry into a pillow to stifle the sound, my body wracked with sobs. How could I not love her as they did? She was so tiny and beautiful and seemed to have the sweetest disposition; even Freedom was enchanted by her.

Izzy knocks on the door and as she enters I do not try to hide my tears. 'Michael is upset that you haven't named her yet.'

It was true, she had been in this world for five days I hadn't agreed on a name for the girl.

'What's wrong with me, Izzy? I can't do this.'

At this point she wakes up crying and I feel as though I could sleep for a thousand years, even though that is mostly all I done since her birth.

'Mother wants to see you in the rose garden.'

I begin to shake my head in protest, but Izzy interrupts me, saying she will feed the baby, knowing I would not miss that opportunity.

As she picks her up from her bassinet, cooing and singing to her as though she had borne a thousand children, I make as much fuss as possible slipping on my pyjama bottoms and pulling a long jumper over my head.

I walk slowly downstairs, passing Michael as he goes to her room with a baby monitor in one hand and a bottle in the other.

'I thought you were sleeping.'

'I was,' I tell him, still vexed that I had been persuaded to go and see Mother.

'Anna, we need to give our daughter a name. Please.'

He looks at me so mournfully that I almost stop

and go back to her with him, but something makes me turn around and continue the slow decent down the staircase.

***

Lillian is carefully pruning her favourite roses and has set a folding chair out for me. I sit down thankfully, holding my painful abdomen as Freedom fusses about me.

'I thought you might need some fresh air,' she tells me, tenderly snipping away dead leaves from the beautiful deep orange roses.

'I remember the day you planted that, Mother. Why is it so special to you?'

My mother looks at me with surprise and smiles, 'It's special because of the time in my life that I planted it. They're called Remember Me roses. *You* can't possibly recall that day, Anna, you weren't born until two years later.'

I scrunch my face up against the low setting sun and tell her crossly, 'I *do* remember. You were wearing a blue dress with white flowers on it, and your lip was bleeding. You were very sad ...'

My confident voice trails away as she searches my face with bewildered eyes, and I sense gentle vibrations gathering in abundance all around me. They ebb over me like strengthening waves, crashing memories that belong to another world.

I leave her alone by the roses and begin to run towards the house, intensifying echoes and whispers resonating from somewhere deep within me.

'*Remember me.*'

I'd heard that voice before, a distant memory or dream of another world. A place I learned a little of purpose, where someone spoke to me of progression and promise.

Despite the ache in my troubled heart, and the familiar pang of fear that I was simply not enough, or that I could never be everything anyone expected I should be, the dark cloud above me seemed to lift a little – just enough for me to feel the welcome reprieve of the mid-morning sun, a gentle breeze lifting the newly grown hair from my face. I take the stairs two at once, and push through the door to find Michael looking at me expectantly.

I run to his side and take the contented little girl from his arms. I want to love her as they do, and show her she is part of my world.

'Hope,' I say softly, as I look down and her blue eyes meet mine. 'She's called Hope.'

THE END

With Special Thanks to

The Accent YA Editor Squad

Aishu Reddy

Alice Brancale

Amani Kabeer-Ali

Anisa Hussain

Barooj Maqsood

Ellie McVay

Grace Morcous

Katie Treharne

Miriam Roberts

Rebecca Freese

Sadie Howorth

Sanaa Morley

Sonali Shetty

With Special Thanks to
The Accent YA Blog Squad

With Special Thanks to

The Accent YA Blog Squad

James Williams

Jayana Jain

Jemima Osborne

Joshua A.P

Karen Bultiauw

Katie Lumsden

Katie Treharne

Kieran Lowley

Kirsty Oconner

Laura Metcalfe

Lois Acari

Maisie Allen

Mariam Khan

Philippa Lloyd

Rachel Abbie

Rebecca Parkinson

Savannah Mullings-Johnson

Sofia Matias

Sophie Hawthorn

Toni Davis

Yolande Branch

THE DEEPEST CUT
natalie flynn

'You haven't said a single word since you've been here. Is it on purpose?' I tried to answer David but I couldn't ... my brain wanted to speak but my throat wouldn't cooperate...

Adam blames himself for his best friend's death. After attempting suicide, he is put in the care of a local mental health facility. There, too traumatized to speak, he begins to write notebooks detailing the events leading up to Jake's murder, trying to understand who is really responsible and cope with how needless it was as a petty argument spiralled out of control and peer pressure took hold.

EIDOLON
SOFI CROFT

Paul is in trouble – moved from a young offenders' prison
to a hospital for the mentally ill because he sees and talks
to his dead sister. He knows she's real. And she has
something important to say.

The doctors' methods are painful and disturbing. As the
treatments build up, Paul is increasingly confused about
what is real and who he can trust.

But he is not the only patient – not the only one who hears
voices that seem connected to strange and inexplicable
powers. When some of his friends are transferred to the
mysterious Ty Eidolon, Paul becomes suspicious that they
are destined for a sinister fate.